From the tennis court  boxing ring to the hock full of blunderful mom

Q. What made the sla nati basketball player Brian Williams so embarrassing?

A. The ball missed the hoop and hit the ref on the head.

★

Q. What did a Canadian soccer team get in return when it traded one of its own players?

A. A soccer ball.

★

Q. Why was jockey Willie Shoemaker's 1957 Kentucky Derby celebration so shameful?

A. He hadn't crossed the finish line yet.

★

Q. What happened to the ball in the wildest throw ever in a professional bowling tournament?

A. It hit the ceiling!

★

Q. What is the shortest career in the history of pro boxing?

A. Fourteen seconds, set by Ace Falu.

★

Q. What was the score of the most boring basketball game in high school history?

A. Georgetown High 1, Homer High 0.

Books by Bruce Nash and Allan Zullo

THE BASEBALL HALL OF SHAME™: Young Fans' Edition
THE FOOTBALL HALL OF SHAME™: Young Fans' Edition
THE SPORTS HALL OF SHAME™: Young Fans' Edition
THE BASEBALL HALL OF SHAME™ 2: Young Fans' Edition

Available from ARCHWAY Paperbacks

THE SPORTS HALL OF SHAME™
YOUNG FANS' EDITION

BRUCE NASH and ALLAN ZULLO
BERNIE WARD, CURATOR

AN ARCHWAY PAPERBACK
Published by POCKET BOOKS

New York   London   Toronto   Sydney   Tokyo   Singapore

AN ARCHWAY PAPERBACK *Original*

An Archway Paperback published by
POCKET BOOKS, a division of Simon & Schuster Inc.
1230 Avenue of the Americas, New York, NY 10020

ISBN: 0-671-69355-7

First Archway Paperback printing August 1990

10 9 8 7 6 5 4 3 2

THE SPORTS HALL OF SHAME is a registered
trademark of Nash and Zullo Productions, Inc.

AN ARCHWAY PAPERBACK and colophon are
registered trademarks of Simon & Schuster Inc.

Printed in the U.S.A.

IL 5+

To my friend Mack McKenzie, for believing that shame is the funniest part of the game.

—B.N.

To Paul Hamann, a true sport and a darn good kid.

—A.Z.

ACKNOWLEDGMENTS

We wish to thank all the fans, athletes, coaches, and sportswriters who contributed nominations.

We are especially grateful to those athletes, past and present, who shared a few laughs with us as they recalled the outrageous moments that earned them a place in The Sports Hall of SHAME.

This book couldn't have been completed without the outstanding research efforts of Al Kermisch. We also appreciate the special efforts of Dusty Brandel, American Auto Racing Writers and Broadcasters Association; Fritz Brennecke; Bob Cicero; Dick Cohen, Sports Bookshelf; Camil Derouches, Montreal Canadiens; Jim Dressel, editor, *Bowlers Journal;* Fred Duckett; F. P. E. Gardner, professor, Eton College, London; Nick Gates, sports editor, *Knoxville Journal;* Max Grizzard; Fred Grossman, editor, *Daily Racing Form;* John Halligan, New York Rangers; Randy Heath; Hiram Henriquez; Billy House; W. Lloyd Johnson, executive director, Society for American Baseball Research; Hank Kaplan, boxing historian; Bill Kiser, National Motorsports Press Association; Ladies Professional Bowling Tour; Dave Lancer, PGA Tour; Jeff Letoffsku; Jerry Levine; Bernie Manhoff, National Veteran Boxers Association; Valarie McGonigle, Atlantic City Race Track; Dick Mittman,

ACKNOWLEDGMENTS

Indianapolis News; Don Naman, Alabama International Motor Speedway; Dave Phillips, major league umpire, and director of officiating, Missouri Valley Conference; Bruce Pluckhahn, curator, National Bowling Hall of Fame and Museum; Pro Bowlers Association; Bob Robinson, *Portland Oregonian;* Carmen Salvino; Beth Shetzeley, U.S. Tennis Association; Luke Soler; Glen Stout, Boston Public Library; Jerry Tapp, associate editor, *Referee* magazine; Steve Waid, *Grand National Scene;* David Wallechinsky, author *The Complete Book of the Olympics;* Joe Whitlock, Motor Sports, Inc.; Tim Williams, NFL Alumni Association; and Howard Willman, *Track & Field News.*

Our lineup wouldn't be such a winner without our rookies, Robyn and Jennifer Nash, and Allison and Sasha Zullo.

CONTENTS

CONTENTS

THE SPORTS
HALL OF SHAME™
YOUNG FANS' EDITION

The Shame Game

After paying a lighthearted tribute to the national pastime in *The Baseball Hall of SHAME: Young Fans' Edition,* and to America's favorite spectator sport in *The Football Hall of SHAME: Young Fans' Edition,* we knew we couldn't stop writing about hilarious happenings and incidents. We had a duty—an obligation—to go beyond the diamond and gridiron. We had to find more outrageous foul-ups and dishonor them in *The Sports Hall of SHAME: Young Fans' Edition.*

Let's face it, baseball and football don't have an exclusive on shame. We found plenty of bloopers, blunders, and buffoonery on the courts, on the ice and in the ring, on the fairways and straightaways, in alleys, on tracks, at high schools and the Olympics. But we haven't forgotten baseball and football in this book. Since these two sports keep giving fans such wacky moments, we have included chapters featuring a new slate of players inducted into The Baseball and Football Halls of SHAME.

Some of The Sports Hall of SHAME inductees—and many of our readers—have asked us if we plan to erect our own Hall of SHAME building. We're trying to find the right place for our shrine, a place that best reflects what we stand for. Among the towns we're considering are Embarrass, Minnesota, and Defeated, Tennessee.

We're also looking into the possibility of buying a parcel of land to incorporate into a burg called Blooperstown.

We imagine a tacky and flashy shrine. We would display some of the mementoes of shameful incidents highlighted in *The Sports Hall of SHAME*. We could show off the thumbtacks that helped pro receiver Rick Eber catch passes. The basketball that the Sacramento Kings couldn't score a hoop with during an entire period. The boxing gloves worn by Joseph "Ace" Falu, whose entire ring career lasted 14 seconds. One of the wheels that flew off racer David Pearson's car when he left the pit too soon. The ball that pro bowler Palmer Fallgren dented the ceiling with. The uniform worn by outfielder Mel Hall that snagged on a wire fence and hung him up, and the skis that flew off the feet of jumper Chuck Ryan in midflight.

Meanwhile, we will go on keeping track of the rib-tickling, embarrassing moments in sports as they happen. We won't play favorites. We will continue to dishonor both the heroes and the zeroes. As our motto says, "Fame *and* shame are part of the game."

DEREK HARPER
Guard ★ Dallas Mavericks ★ May 6, 1984

In NBA games, teams usually score a combined total of more than 200 points. So what's the big deal if a player loses track of just one? Ask Derek Harper.

His moment came in a crucial 1984 playoff game against the Los Angeles Lakers. The Dallas Mavericks' rookie guard thought his team was ahead by a point, so he dribbled the final six seconds off the clock and started celebrating. Then he was told to look at the scoreboard. The score was tied 108–108! His blunder sent the game into overtime, where the Lakers ripped the Mavericks 122–115. L.A. jumped ahead three-games-to-one and went on to win the playoff series.

The Mavericks were playing at home against the favored Lakers and badly needed a victory to even the playoff series at two wins apiece. It was a nip-and-tuck battle. With 31 seconds left, Dallas center Pat Cummings sank a left-handed hook shot. It tied the score at 108–108, but Cummings was fouled by Magic Johnson.

The Mavericks had no timeouts left. While Harper talked with coach Dick Motta, Cummings tried the free

3

throw. It would have given Dallas the lead, but Cummings missed. Somehow, Harper thought his teammate made the shot to put Dallas ahead 109–108.

The Lakers rebounded the missed free throw and worked the ball in to Kareem Abdul-Jabbar. He tried a sky hook, but missed, and the Mavericks grabbed the rebound. They had time to get off one shot, or at least try to draw the foul. The Mavericks pushed the ball up the court and passed to Harper, who dribbled forty feet from the basket without being bothered. At the buzzer, he began celebrating over what he thought was his team's biggest victory in its short four-year history. Then the network TV cameras showed Harper's horror when he realized he had messed up royally. They needed a crane to pick up his jaw.

Motta, who tried everything to alert Harper, said afterward, "When I saw Derek backing up, it hit me that he didn't know the score or the time. I wanted to tackle him. Would they call a foul on a coach for tackling one of his players?"

Added Los Angeles coach Pat Riley, "I was as surprised as anybody when Harper didn't go in. Why, I was about to call a play for him myself."

A mob of reporters rushed Harper's locker after the game. He said, "I'll take the blame for the loss. It was a mistake. I thought we were ahead."

The way Harper works with numbers, it's a good bet he'd never land a job as an accountant.

BRIAN WILLIAMS

Guard ★ University of Cincinnati ★ Jan. 19, 1977

It was bad enough that Brian Williams missed the entire basket on a slam dunk. Even worse, he wound up hitting an official squarely on the head.

The 6-foot, 5-inch Cincinnati guard made the wackiest dunk in college basketball history. It happened during a game against the University of Louisville.

"I've seen some missed dunks, but never one where a referee got conked," recalled Williams' coach, Gale Catlett. "Brian really nailed him. That official staggered all over the court for at least a couple of minutes."

The visiting Bearcats were then rated No. 2 in the nation. They were trailing Louisville by six points with two minutes left in the game. Williams soared down the lane and launched himself for what looked like a dramatic slam dunk. Meanwhile, referee Darwin Brown positioned himself under the basket.

Williams sailed high in the air, held the ball straight over his head, and then slammed it down. But he missed both the rim and the backboard. In fact, he missed everything—except the referee. The ball smashed into Brown's head and bounced crazily into the seats.

"The crowd loved it, but I nearly got knocked out," Brown recalled. "I staggered around and had the same thought as everyone else—how could he miss the basket like that?"

FRED BROWN

Guard ★ Georgetown Hoyas ★ March 29, 1982

In all of collegiate national championship action, no blunder is so clear in fans' minds as the shockingly bad pass made by Fred Brown of the Georgetown Hoyas.

With eight seconds left in the 1982 championship clash, the Hoyas had the ball. But the North Carolina Tar Heels had the lead, 63–62. Brown, the usually reliable guard, rushed the ball upcourt. He was determined to get it to one of his teammates for the final game-winning basket.

He saw that Sleepy Floyd was covered, along with Patrick Ewing and Ed Spriggs. "I should have called timeout, but I decided to pass it to Eric Smith, who was on the right side of the lane," Brown recalled. "I thought I saw Smitty out of the right corner of my eye. But it wasn't him."

No, it was North Carolina's James Worthy. Brown fired a perfect chest-high pass that went right into the hands of a surprised but happy Worthy. He clutched the ball and then dribbled the other way. With two seconds left in the game, he was deliberately fouled. Worthy missed both free throws, but it didn't matter. Georgetown lost 63–62.

"Worthy didn't steal it—I gave it away," said Brown. "My peripheral vision is pretty good, but this time it failed me. It was only a split second. But that's all it takes to lose a game. I knew it was bad as soon as I let it go. If I'd had a rubber band, I would have yanked it back in."

KEVIN DOHERTY
Guard ★ Davidson College ★ Jan. 5, 1976

Some college basketball players go through all four years of school without any recognition. Kevin Doherty gained fame in just 38 seconds. That's how long it took him to rack up *four* personal fouls.

The second-string sophomore guard for the Davidson College Wildcats was on the bench. The visiting University of Virginia Cavaliers were pulling steadily away from his team midway through the second half. Suddenly, Davidson coach Bo Brickels called Doherty over, and said, "Get in there and make something happen."

The coach was thinking along the lines of inspired play. What he saw instead was foul play.

Doherty started to bring the ball upcourt. Only two seconds after he first touched it, he was called for charging. He picked up his second personal foul—on defense—just 14 seconds later. Seventeen seconds after that, he hacked Virginia's Billy Langloh on the arm for his third foul. A few seconds later, Langloh stole the ball from Doherty and went in for a lay-up. He paid the price as Doherty shoved him against the basketball standards. Only 38 seconds had ticked off the clock and already Doherty had tallied four personal fouls. It was an amazing record for speed, although the NCAA doesn't officially keep track of such things.

"Kevin fouled guys so fast that no one realized what had happened," recalled Brickels. Doherty finally managed to control himself for over four minutes before committing his fifth foul. He was whistled to the bench just 5:06 after he had entered the game.

"It was a night to remember," recalled Doherty. "Or was it a night to forget?" In a classic understatement, he added, "In that game, I may have been a mite too aggressive."

CHUCK CONNORS
Center ★ Boston Celtics ★ Nov. 5, 1946

Chuck Connors made a smashing debut in front of bleachers full of Boston Celtics fans during the team's very first home game. He shattered the glass backboard.

Years before he starred in the TV series *The Rifleman,* Connors played pro basketball. He made Boston's roster in 1946, the team's first season.

At the Celtics' home opener, more than 4,000 fans crowded into the Boston Arena to see the league's newest team take on the Chicago Stags. The spectators didn't know all the Celtics. But they soon took special note of the squad's 6-foot, 5-inch center.

Connors got their attention during pregame warm-ups. Just five minutes before the tip-off, he tossed up a shot. It hit the rim of the basket, and the backboard leaned forward. Like a spiderweb, it broke into a million pieces.

Arena officals raced over to the Boston Garden and borrowed one of its backboards. Then they raced back to the Arena and set it up. The game was delayed for more than an hour.

"The crowd got pretty fidgety after a while and [Celtics coach] Honey Russell was incensed," recalled Connors. "Boy, did he let me have it. He shouted,

Chuck Connors rifles a pass after his "smashing" debut.

'Connors, every time you're around me, something bad happens!' I told him, 'It was just a set shot and it's not really my fault.' And he replied, 'You threw it up there, didn't you?' He just jumped all over me, and the longer it took to get a new backboard, the madder he got.

"Of all the times for it to happen, it had to be at the very first Celtics game. They had been ballyhooing the new team and the game, and of course the fans were all excited. Then I had to break the backboard. There I was, standing around, and everybody was pointing the finger at me for holding things up. As far as I was concerned, it was just an inferior backboard. But I sure got the blame for it."

Once the game began, Connors tried to make the crowd forget the long delay. He played tough defense and scored eight points, but that wasn't enough. Chicago nipped Boston 57–55.

"It's fun talking about the shattered backboard now, but back then I was looking for a place to hide," said Connors. "Can you imagine what today's Celtics fans would do to you if you delayed one of their precious games like that?"

BUTCH MORGAN
Coach ★ College of St. Joseph the Provider
Dec. 11, 1974

Before a big game, Coach Butch Morgan read his team a poem he hoped would lead them to victory. Unfortunately, the verse did just the reverse.

The St. Joseph cagers of Rutland, Vermont, were about to tangle with their more powerful rival, Castleton State College. Morgan tried to fire up his players with a poem called "Don't Quit." He made copies of it and gave one to each player. Then he read it out loud.

"After I read the poem to them, I asked their response to it," recalled Morgan. "I took a few extra minutes to make sure each player had the chance to study the poem and talk about it. The gym was jammed and the fans were waiting for us to come out. The ref kept coming into the locker room telling us to get out on the floor and I kept telling him we weren't done yet. I felt what I was doing in the locker room was more important than what was going to happen on the court, anyway."

The refs obviously weren't poetry fans. When St. Joseph finally came out onto the floor, they were charged with five technical fouls. Each starting player got one—for delaying the game. Castleton's Dave Bove shot five technical free throws before the clock even started. He made three of them, and they turned out to be big points. St. Joseph lost 79–78.

Even though they lost because of the poem, Morgan was happy. He called the game "the high point" of his coaching career. "I expected my team to get beat by 15 or 20 points, yet those kids played a phenomenal game. In all honesty," added Morgan, "they probably would have won it—with a little bit of decent coaching."

UNIVERSITY OF CALIFORNIA AT SANTA CRUZ SEA LIONS
Jan. 8, 1982

If the Indians at the Battle of Little Big Horn had played basketball for the University of California at Santa Cruz, Custer's Last Stand would never have happened.

In this foul-filled game, the Sea Lions' opponents were reduced to a "team" of one. Yet Cal–Santa Cruz still couldn't overtake him. By himself, he scored five points in the final two minutes and saved the game.

Midway through the second half, Cal–Santa Cruz was trailing the West Coast Christian College Knights by 15 points. Then the Knights got into serious foul trouble. Because of injuries, they had suited up only eight players. In a game officiated by whistle-happy refs, it turned out eight wasn't enough. When the fourth Knight fouled out, the Sea Lions had a five- to four-man edge. But they still couldn't narrow the lead—even when more West Coast Christian players fouled out. Finally, with 2:10 left to play, West Coast Christian was down to its last man, junior Mike Lockhart, a 6-foot, 1-inch guard. Under NCAA rules, a game can continue when a team has only one player left—if that team is leading or has a chance to win.

Lockhart's coach, Jerry Turner, called timeout to talk with the officials. Then he explained the rules to Lockhart. The guard could inbound the ball only if an opposing player touched it. The coach's final words to Lockhart were, "Don't foul."

A foul would have ended the game. Lockhart had

four personals and there was no one left to replace him. The Sea Lions were in much better shape. Four of their starters had fouled out, but they had nine players on the team.

Lockhart found himself alone on the floor against the Sea Lions with West Coast Christian leading 70–57. "I was scared to death," he said. "I had confidence in my ball handling, but I had four fouls myself and there was nobody to pass to. The coach told me to calm down and take my time."

If the Sea Lions were going to close the 13-point gap, it had to be now. In those final two minutes, they played five-on-one basketball. But they had never practiced any plays for this situation. So they acted like they didn't know what to do. One player was called for traveling on a lay-up. Another got whistled for a three-second lane violation. "Nothing seemed to go right for them," recalled Turner. "Their players were fighting over the shots. It was chaos."

Said Cal–Santa Cruz coach Joe Richardson, "On offense, we tried planting a player under our basket and heaving the ball downcourt to him, but the pass went wild. We also tried working it down with shorter passes. But in the excitement, another pass went out of bounds."

Meanwhile, Lockhart did what he could. He rolled the ball inbounds and jogged alongside. He then waited for an opponent to touch it so he could snatch it back. He recovered another inbounds pass by bouncing the ball off an opponent's leg. The Sea Lions were so bad, they let Lockhart grab a rebound from them. He even blocked one shot against a player who was five inches taller than he was. It nearly gave his coach heart failure. "I was afraid he might have been called for a foul on the play," said Turner. Afterward, he shouted to Lockhart to lay off the shot-blocking routine.

When he had the ball, Lockhart managed to eat up time by weaving his way through the Cal–Santa Cruz defense until he was fouled. He made five of six free throws.

"Our biggest mistake was fouling him," said Richardson. "It was just unintelligent on our part. But I suppose my players became frustrated when they couldn't get the ball from him."

Despite their four-man advantage, the Sea Lions scored only ten points and gave up five. It wasn't nearly enough to overcome the 13-point deficit. They lost 75–67.

ANDY LANDERS
Women's Basketball Coach ★ University of Georgia
1974

When it comes to coaching tactics, Andy Landers' method ranks at the top for shame.

Whenever he thinks his team's defense is rotten, he gives a stinker of an order. His players' practice uniforms go unwashed until he sees better defense. Even if it takes weeks.

The Lady Bulldogs have worn dirty, smelly uniforms several times during his 18-year career. Landers, who believes defense is the key to winning, remembers coming up with the B.O. M.O. after one really frustrating game. "I told the team, 'Hey, our defense stinks. As

The Lady Bulldogs get a whiff of their stinky duds.

long as it stinks, we're going to stink, too. Until you start playing defense the way it is meant to be played, we're not going to wash any of your practice stuff.' That caught their attention. It's worked every time since.

"When they pull on that rancid uniform every day, they're reminded why they stink so badly. If they don't come out and give me a better effort defensively, they'll just keep smelling badly."

The last time Landers dropped his stink bomb announcement was in 1986. The Lady Bulldogs were 15–1 and ranked second in the nation at the time. But Landers was still disgusted with their defensive performance, so he banned the washing of their practice uniforms for nearly three weeks. On the advice of the team trainer, however, the players' socks were not included in the laundry ban.

"We've been stinking it up pretty good, in more ways than one," Landers told the press after two weeks. After the defense improved in practice, he declared, "If we can play a few games like we've been practicing, we'll throw those babies in the washing machine."

A week later, the uniforms were sent to the laundry, and the players finally breathed a little easier. They lost only one more game the rest of the year, and finished second in the nation with a sweet-smelling record of 30–2.

SACRAMENTO KINGS
Feb. 4, 1987

In the worst first-quarter performance in pro basketball history, the Sacramento Kings missed every single shot from the floor.

The last-place Kings were playing in the Forum against the first-place Los Angeles Lakers. The Kings looked like they had all flunked Basket Weaving 101. They couldn't make a basket in 18 tries in the opening period. No jams, no jumpers, no sky hooks. No tip-ins, no three-point bombs—no nothing.

After the first 12 minutes, the scoreboard read: Lakers—40, Kings—4. Sacramento scored fewer points in the first quarter than any team since the introduction of the 24-second clock in 1954.

Kings coach Phil Johnson called a timeout 2:11 into the game. Already the Lakers had jumped out to a 10–0 lead. Two minutes later the score was 16–0. Chick Hearn, the Lakers' announcer, set a record for the earliest prediction of an NBA victory. He told his listeners, "This game is in the refrigerator." Meanwhile, Johnson had called his second timeout to regroup his troops. It didn't help. Los Angeles guard Byron Scott's breakaway jam made it 22–0. Johnson was forced to use his third timeout at 5:26.

With 2:54 left in the period, Sacramento was behind by an unbelievable 29–0 score. Then the Kings' Derek Smith was fouled. The pressure was on. Could he do what no one else on his team could do? Could he put the ball through the hoop? Smith eyed the basket as if this were a possible game-winning foul shot. He took a deep breath and tossed the ball through the basket. Sacramento had its first point. The Laker crowd went wild and gave Smith a standing ovation.

The Kings' entire offense in the opening period came from the charity line where they managed to sink four foul shots. The quarter ended with the Lakers leading by ten times Sacramento's tally, 40–4.

The Kings didn't score a two-pointer until their 22nd attempt. Eddie Johnson finally banked in a three-footer 20 seconds into the second period. The ice was broken. Sacramento then played L.A. even the rest of the way and lost 128–92.

"In the eighth grade something like this happened to me," said Derek Smith. "We scored like 14 points, and the other guys had 80. I remember I cried for a few days after that. You can't do that here. But the Lakers toyed with us like we were little kids.

"When you're down 10–0 to the Lakers, you know it's getting bad. When it's 16–0, you know it's real bad. When it's 22–0, you're critical, and they might as well pull the plug."

17

JOE SOSKOVIC
Referee ★ Feb. 12, 1978

Referee Joe Soskovic was such a stickler for the rules that he called a technical foul for joyfulness—after the game was over.

His uncalled-for call turned a 70–69 victory into an unfair 2–0 forfeit defeat.

The 8–10 Southern Connecticut Owls were beating the highly favored 13–5 Springfield College Chiefs 70–69 with five seconds left in the game. Then Southern Connecticut's Daryl Breland stole the ball at midcourt. He dribbled toward his basket until time ran out and the buzzer sounded.

To celebrate his team's upset victory, Breland tried to slam dunk the ball. Unfortunately, he did it right in front of Soskovic. The ref believed this normal response to a hard-fought win was against the rules. Even though time had expired and the coaches were shaking each other's hands, Soskovic called a technical foul on Breland.

Soskovic claimed the game wasn't over until he and the official scorer approved the final score. Breland had dunked the ball before that happened. So Soskovic charged him with a violation—dunking a dead ball. For this awful crime, Springfield's Don Lemieux was allowed a technical foul shot. He made it, tying the score at 70 and sending the game into overtime.

Southern Connecticut coach Ed Brown was furious at Soskovic. He declared that his team had won fair and square. The insulted, angry coach refused to put his team back on the floor. "As far as I'm concerned, we won the game," Brown said later. "With all due conscience, I couldn't continue to play. So I told my kids, 'Let's go. The game is over.' Then we started running off the floor." Soskovic responded by awarding Springfield a 2–0 forfeit victory.

The ref didn't have to worry about getting booed off the court because the game was played at Springfield's Memorial Field House. He also had some further support when, during all the fuss, he conferred with Dr. Edward Steitz. Dr. Steitz was the editor of the rule book of the International Association of Approved Basketball Officials. He also just happened to be the athletic director of Springfield College. "As far as I'm concerned, the official called it by the book," said Steitz.

The Owls filed a formal protest, but the Eastern College Athletic Conference disallowed it, claiming that "technically, the official's call was correct."

Since the officials were so stuck on details, they should have ruled in favor of Southern Connecticut. Technically, Breland didn't dunk the ball. He missed the basket! "It wasn't a dunk because he never reached the rim," said Coach Brown. "The ball never went into the basket."

Randy Smith
Guard ★ Buffalo Braves ★ 1973

As a young guard for the NBA's Buffalo Braves, Randy Smith learned how to play tough defense and run the offense. But he never quite learned how to call timeouts.

"He used to do things you wouldn't believe," said Jack Ramsay, then coach of the Braves. Smith later became a two-time All-Star, averaging 17.4 points per game in ten seasons. But early in his career, he gave Ramsay fits.

Recalling a game against the Milwaukee Bucks, Ramsay said, "The Bucks ran off six straight points, so I wanted a timeout. Randy was bringing the ball up and I yelled, 'Randy, timeout!' He just left the ball in the middle of his dribble and came over. He forgot to call it."

Randy pulled another dandy later that same year during a game against the Golden State Warriors in San Francisco. The Braves were trying to break a seven-game losing streak. That night, Buffalo played well and Smith scored 13 points in the third quarter. As a result, the Braves took a 79–67 lead into the fourth period.

But the Warriors launched a furious rally and closed the margin to 99–97 in the final minute. Then Golden State covered the Braves with a full-court press and Randy had trouble finding an open teammate. With the clock ticking down and the crowd screaming, Coach Ramsay yelled at Smith to call a timeout.

Now how hard could that be? All Randy had to do was follow five simple steps: (1) Hold onto the ball. (2) Turn to the ref. (3) Say, "Timeout." (4) Wait for the official to award the timeout. (5) Flip him the ball. It's incredible, but Smith skipped steps 1, 3, and 4. With the game on the line, Randy casually turned to referee Mendy Rudolph. He tossed him the ball without ever calling time. Rudolph quickly jumped out of the way. The loose ball was picked up by Jeff Mullins of the

Warriors, who drove right in for a lay-up to tie the score.

Buffalo's Bob McAdoo didn't give Smith another chance to goof up. He called for—and got—a timeout. "I was beside myself," Coach Ramsay recalled. "I said, 'Randy, what are you doing?' He looked puzzled and said, 'Coach, the ref *knew* I was throwing it to him.'"

The Braves never recovered from Smith's blunder. They went on to lose their eighth straight, 106–101.

LEE TREVINO
British Open ★ July 12, 1970

St. Andrews is the birthplace of golf—and the site of Lee Trevino's biggest blunder.

Going into the final round of the 1970 British Open, Super Mex had a total score of 207. He held a three-stroke edge over Jack Nicklaus, Doug Sanders, and Tony Jacklin, who were tied for second at 210.

But Trevino slipped badly and quickly lost his lead. What finally beat him was the big boner he pulled on the fifth hole. What makes this hole special is its huge, unusual double green with two cups for two separate holes. Trevino had played the hole three times in the tournament. But the fourth time around, his usual alertness faded like a sliced drive.

Trevino pulled an iron out of his bag for the approach shot, studied the green, and sent the ball straight for the flag. But it was the wrong flag! The ball landed on the green—but 80 feet away from the right hole. The moment he hit it, Trevino slapped his forehead like one of the Three Stooges and said, "I done hit to the wrong stick!" Then he added, "And I'm just dumb enough to have done it, too."

Lee Trevino: "I done hit to the wrong stick!"

Trevino three-putted for a bogey. Meanwhile, Nicklaus and Sanders pulled away from the pack. Trevino never recovered from his goof and wound up watching Nicklaus win the British Open in a playoff against Sanders.

RAY AINSLEY
U.S. Open ★ June 10, 1938

Ray Ainsley holds the record for the most incredible score in the U.S. Open. He shot a 19—on one hole!

Ever since then, Ainsley has been the patron saint of duffers the world over.

Ray carded a triple-triple-triple-triple-triple bogey. He did it on the par four 16th hole at Denver's Cherry Hills Country Club during the second round of the

23

1938 Open. The young Californian, who was playing in his first Open, had been shooting decent golf, although he was never a contender. He should have been just another name in a long list of qualifiers. But instead, he swung his way to shame on one hole.

Ainsley got into instant trouble when he hooked his drive into the rough. That set him up for disaster. His second shot dropped into a shallow, but swift-moving creek in front of the green. Ray saw that the ball was on a sand bar a few inches under the clear, cold water. He decided he had a playable lie. Playable for a trout, maybe, but not a golfer.

Nevertheless, Ainsley took off his shoes and socks, drew a blaster out of his bag, and planted his feet in the creek. Just as he started to swing, the current moved the ball downstream a few inches. He hit nothing but water and sand. So he took a new stance and swung again . . . and again . . . and again. Ray missed each time as the current pushed the ball farther and farther away. He leaped about the creek, flailing away at the ball with his iron. Ainsley was soaked and splattered with sand, but he refused to give up.

Ray's playing partner, Bud McKinney, stood on the bank with his fist jammed in his mouth to keep from laughing. But official scorer Red Anderson was calling the strokes out loud. After the count reached nine, Anderson couldn't control himself. He fell on the ground in stitches, and told McKinney between guffaws, "Take over the count, Bud."

So McKinney dutifully shouted, "Ten! . . . Eleven! . . . Twelve! . . ."

Ainsley finally nailed the ball—on his 13th stroke. It soared out of the water like a missile—a misguided one. The ball crashed into a clump of bushes well beyond the green. Never-say-die Ray worked his way through the brush and found it. It took *three* more whacks before the ball plopped onto the green. Then, as if a sixth sense told him that he could break the old record of 18, Ainsley three-putted. The record was his—the worst score ever for one hole in a pro championship.

"And everybody loved him for it," wrote Chester Nelson, sports editor of *The Rocky Mountain News,* who was covering the tournament. Nelson said Ray's record was applauded by "all the dubs [boneheads] who ever forgot to touch second base, all the dubs who ever ran backwards in the last quarter, and all the other dubs."

GARY PLAYER
Huddersfield, England ★ June 12, 1955

In one of the most shameful shots in golf history, Gary Player was knocked out by his own ball.

It was the young South African pro's first trip to England. He was battling for the lead in a tournament at Huddersfield, England. Teeing it up for the final hole, he needed a par four to win and a bogey five to tie.

Player hooked his drive into the rough. His second shot landed to the right of the green only a few inches away from a stone wall. He couldn't just chip the ball onto the green because there wasn't enough room for his backswing. Gary didn't want to waste a stroke tapping it clear before chipping.

That's when he came up with what he figured was a brilliant idea. He'd bounce the ball off the wall like a pool player hitting a bank shot. Gary decided exactly where the ball should hit so it would rebound onto the green.

"I tried to be fancy," wrote Player years ago. "The ball came off the wall in fine shape, but instead of finishing on the green, it ricocheted back and hit me on the cheek. The force of the blow actually knocked me cold momentarily.

"Finally, I regained my senses, at least a portion of them. Still groggy, I chipped onto the green and then somehow knocked the long putt into the hole."

Gary gave a sigh of relief. He believed he was tied for the lead and would be in a playoff. Instead, an official informed Player that he had earned a two-stroke penalty. He had impeded the flight of the ball because it had struck him. Thus, Gary lost the tournament by taking it on the chin.

BOBBY CRUICKSHANK
U.S. Open ★ June 9, 1934

Bobby Cruickshank lost the 1934 U.S. Open when he threw his club—not in anger, but in joy.

He did it in the final round at the Merion Country Club near Philadelphia. At the turn, the small, wiry Scot had a two-stroke lead and was shooting for a par four on the 378-yard 11th hole. After hitting a decent drive, he swatted a weak approach shot. To his dismay, the ball fell into the creek running in front of the green.

Bobby Cruickshank sees nothing but birdies.

The gallery groaned as the shot sent up a huge splash of water. But suddenly the crowd broke into wild cheers as the ball bounced out of the water and landed on the green just ten feet from the pin. The ball had been saved from a watery grave by sheer luck—it had hit the only submerged flat rock in the stream.

Bobby was overcome with joy. He tossed his club into the air, tipped his cap, and shouted, "Thank you, God!" While he continued to celebrate, he failed to watch his club. He didn't notice it was falling—until it conked him on the noggin and knocked him to the ground! He saw more birdies than he made during the whole tournament.

The dazed golfer managed to get back on his feet, and two-putted for a par. But Cruickshank never fully recovered from being clubbed by his own club. He was only able to make par twice on the next seven holes, and tumbled from first place to a third-place finish.

LLOYD MANGRUM
U.S. Open ★ June 11, 1950

Lloyd Mangrum got so bugged that he wound up losing the 1950 U.S. Open.

It happened at the Merion Golf Club near Philadelphia. Mangrum was in a playoff battle with Ben Hogan and George Fazio. They were approaching the green on the par four 16th hole with Mangrum trailing by one stroke. Hogan and Fazio were on the green in two. Mangrum, lying in three, desperately needed to sink a 15-footer to save par.

Lining up his putt, Mangrum noticed a gnat resting on his ball. The golfer waited for the insect to fly off, but it didn't. So he marked the ball's position, picked it up, and blew on it. The offending gnat flew off and Mangrum put the ball back. Then he rolled it in for what he thought was a par. Hogan, who was the leader, also parred the hole and Mangrum assumed he was still only one stroke behind.

He was wrong. To his shock, Mangrum learned he was now three strokes behind. Isaac Grainger, chairman of the USGA rules committee, had been sitting in the gallery. Grainger informed Mangrum that he had broken a rule. Lifting a ball that is in play means a penalty of two strokes. As good a pro as Mangrum was, he had never heard of that rule. Now it was too late.

Not knowing the rules took him completely out of the running for the championship. With only two holes remaining, he couldn't overcome his error and he lost the playoff to Ben Hogan.

The Hockey
HALL OF SHAME

STEVE SMITH
Defenseman ★ Edmonton Oilers ★ April 30, 1986

If ever Steve Smith wished the ice could crack beneath his skates and swallow him up, it was in the last period of a deciding game in the 1986 Stanley Cup playoffs.

Smith committed a costly and amazing blunder.

It happened in the seventh and deciding game of the Smythe Division finals in Edmonton where his Oilers were gunning for their third straight Stanley Cup. In the third period, they had rallied from a 2–0 deficit to tie the Calgary Flames 2–2.

Less than six minutes were left in regulation play. Then Smith, the Oilers' rookie defenseman, made the poorest pass in Stanley Cup history. Smith was playing a regular shift because veteran Lee Fogolin was injured. The rookie attempted a routine clearing pass from behind the corner of his own net. But the puck hit Oilers goaltender Grant Fuhr on the back of the ankle and skipped into the Edmonton net for a stunning goal. When Smith realized what he had done, he dropped to his knees and hung his head in shame. Calgary's left wing, Perry Berezan, was the closest opponent to the net, so he was credited with the goal with 5:14

remaining in the game. Fired up by the unexpected goal, the Flames held on for an upset 3–2 victory.

Afterward, in the stunned Oilers' locker room, Smith was teary-eyed. He said, "I just tried to make a quick play with a guy bearing down on me. I got good wood on it. It's just that it didn't go in the direction I wanted. It's the worst feeling I've ever had in my life. Sooner or later I've got to face it. But at least it's not the end of the world."

No, but it was the end of Edmonton's season. The two-time NHL champions were ousted from the Stanley Cup playoffs.

Of all the days to screw up, wouldn't you know it happened on Smith's 23rd birthday? Apparently, he forgot that birthday boys are supposed to receive gifts—not give them.

MONTREAL WANDERERS
February 1906

It took all season for the Montreal Wanderers to win the Stanley Cup. But it took them only a few hours to lose pro hockey's most treasured prize.

Right after winning the championship in 1906, the Wanderers—no relation to the NHL's Canadiens— threw a party. Then they decided to have their photo taken with the coveted silver trophy.

The players went to Jimmy Rice's Famous Studio. They held up the cup, smiled for the cameras, and then started partying. But they forgot all about the very thing they had worked so hard to win. They left the cup behind in a corner of the empty studio.

Apparently, everyone on the team assumed that someone else had the cup. Management didn't realize it was missing until the beginning of the next season. An all-points bulletin was issued throughout Montreal and a mad search for the trophy began.

One of the players recalled last seeing the cup at Jimmy Rice's studio. Rice said he hadn't seen it since the night he took the picture. But the photographer had a hunch. He asked his cleaning lady if she had any idea where the cup might be. After he described it in detail, she said, "Oh, is *that* what it is."

She then explained what happened to the cup. A few hours after the team left, she cleaned up the studio. While doing so, she came across this lovely silver cup. She figured it wasn't doing any good sitting in the corner. So she took it home, where she put it to good, practical use. She filled it with potting soil, planted some geraniums in it, and left it on her windowsill all summer long. Somewhat sadly, the woman returned the trophy to the team—minus the geraniums.

PHILADELPHIA FLYERS VS. BUFFALO SABRES
"The Fog Game"
May 20, 1975

During the third game of the 1975 Stanley Cup finals, the players skated like they were in a fog.

That's because they *were* in a fog. And it was so thick it would have kept the U.S. Navy in port.

The Philadelphia Flyers were visiting the Buffalo

Sabres in a game played under the worst conditions ever in NHL playoff history. First, it was held so late in the season that the weather had turned hot. This was a serious problem because Buffalo's Memorial Stadium was not air-conditioned. As a result, the teams battled in stifling heat and sticky humidity. Patches of ice melted into puddles, spreading a thick, waist-high fog throughout the league's smallest rink.

The game was delayed eleven times because of the pea soup. Each time, the players were sent out to circle the arena and stir up the air. The only players who weren't annoyed by the delays were the benchwarmers. They received more ice time than ever before.

It was one of those you-have-to-see-it-to-believe-it games. Unfortunately, most of the fans at the game *couldn't* see it. They could only hear the puck slapping against the sticks and boards.

As bad as it was for the fans, conditions were worse for the players. The rink was a foggy hotbox that slowed the once-swift skaters. By the end of the game, their legs were too tired to rush the puck up the ice. "It was so bloody hot out there it was unbearable," complained Flyer defenseman Ed Van Impe.

"Some of the guys took their [long john] underwear off after the third period because it was so wet and heavy from sweat," said Flyer assistant coach Barry Ashbee. The heat and fog created a spooky scene. At one point, a small bat swept down from the upper reaches of the arena. It buzzed the rink until Buffalo's Jim Lorentz high-sticked it to death. Then Philly's Rick MacLeish dropped it in the penalty box. It all added yet another weird touch to the already-strange game.

As luck would have it, the Sabres and Flyers wearily

skated into overtime. After 18 more minutes, Buffalo's Gilbert Perreault and Rene Robert came out of the fog. Like phantoms, they skated into the Philadelphia zone just when the Flyers were in the midst of a line change. Perreault fired a shot into the corner, and it ricocheted to Robert, who blasted a 24-footer. Flyers goalie Bernie Parent could barely make out the shadowy figures in the middle of the ice. He never moved. "I didn't have the foggiest notion where the puck was until it was too late," he said. By the time Parent reacted, Robert's slap shot crashed into the net. The Sabres had defeated the Flyers 5–4.

"Four or five times the Sabres came down with the puck and I couldn't see who had it," said Parent. "I'm surprised the game didn't end sooner. I'll put some windshield wipers on my mask for the next time."

The fog returned during the next game, which Buffalo won 4–2 to tie the series. The Sabre management unveiled an unusual, if basic new system for fog control. Five teams of attendants skated around the ice with bed sheets, waving off the fog.

When the Flyers returned home to their air-conditioned Spectrum, they played under better conditions. They drubbed the Sabres in Philadelphia to win the Stanley Cup.

The Buffalo pea soup created a scene like something out of a horror movie. But Philly coach Fred Shero remembered playing under worse conditions in Houston in 1948. "It was so bad," he recalled, "that we were on our hands and knees looking for the puck. We couldn't find it, so they called the game."

JIM STEWART

Goalie ★ Boston Bruins ★ Jan. 10, 1980

It was a good thing Boston Bruins rookie Jim Stewart wore a face mask. It hid his embarrassment after he made the worst NHL debut ever for a goalie.

Bruins regulars Gerry Cheevers and Gilles Gilbert were both sidelined and Boston found itself short of puck stoppers. So the team called up Stewart from Utica of the Eastern League. Just twelve hours later, he was tending the nets against the St. Louis Blues. Stewart had dreamed about this moment ever since he graduated from Holy Cross. He'd imagined snaring slap shots, deflecting rebounds, and making the big save. Unfortunately, his dreams didn't come true.

The way Stewart played was more like a nightmare. The Bruins would have been better off pulling him at the opening face-off. He let three of the first four shots get by him. The Zamboni had barely left the rink before Stewart blew his first chance at a save. Just 1:08 into the game, the Blues' Brian Sutter fired a 55-foot slap shot by Stewart's left. Less than two minutes later, Bernie Federko of St. Louis faked a pass. He deked Stewart out of position and flipped the puck into the net. It took only 51 seconds for the Blues to score again. Mike Crombeen put a backhander through the rookie's legs from up close. In his first three minutes and 46 seconds of NHL goaltending, Stewart had given up three goals.

He settled down and shut out St. Louis for nearly twelve minutes. Then Sutter sailed the puck through Stewart's legs for his second goal of the period. About a minute later, at 16:42, Crombeen nailed his second goal when he whacked in his own rebound.

At the end of the first period, the Bruins trailed 5–2. Stewart had stopped only four of nine shots on goal and Boston coach Fred Creighton had seen more than enough. He replaced Stewart with Marco Baron—another rookie. Baron surrendered two goals in the last two periods in a 7–4 Bruins loss.

In the dressing room after the game, Stewart was surrounded by media people. With three microphones shoved under his chin, he smiled. Then he asked with wide-eyed innocence, "What's it like when we win?"

He claimed he wasn't scared in his debut. "I felt great in the pregame warmups and I didn't think I was nervous, but I must have been. Nothing went right from the first shot on. I couldn't stop a basketball. Three of their goals went through my legs and twice I moved too quickly. It was some kind of a shock to be here."

It certainly was no shock when Stewart was quickly shipped back to Utica. He never played in the NHL again.

NEW YORK RANGERS
Jan. 23, 1944

In the most lopsided score in NHL history, the New York Rangers were clobbered 15–0 by the Detroit Red Wings.

The goal light flashed so often that New York goalie Ken "Tubby" McAuley got a suntan. But his goaltending wasn't to blame as much as the Ranger defense.

They allowed Detroit an incredible 58 shots on goal. To his credit, McAuley stopped 43 of them. To his discredit, he let 15 get by him—the most ever in a single NHL game.

Of course, the 12,293 fans at Detroit's Olympia were thrilled. Almost every player on the Red Wings either scored or got an assist. The only ones who didn't were defenseman Cully Simon and goalie Connie Dion. The Rangers turned losing into an art form. It took Detroit only three minutes to score its first goal. At one point, the Red Wings were short-handed, yet they still passed the puck to each other for 90 seconds without a single Ranger touching it. New York's Bryan Hextall finally got his stick on it. But Detroit's Flash Hollett spun him around with a check. Hollett dished off a quick pass to Bill Quackenbush who slapped in a ten-footer for a 2–0 lead. The rout was on.

In the second period, the Rangers were down 3–0 before they got bombed with four more goals in just six minutes. By the final stanza, McAuley's chances would have been better with a firing squad. At least there, he'd only have been shot at once. The Red Wings fired pucks like they were using machine guns, racking up a never-before-seen eight goals in the third period.

The Detroit fans screamed themselves hoarse shouting for more. They almost got their wish for a 16th goal as the game ended. In the final seconds, three Red Wings broke away without a Ranger between them and McAuley. They passed the puck back and forth to confuse the goalie. But they dallied too long. Just before Carl Liscombe fired point-blank into the net, the green light flashed. The massacre was over.

"I was so mad after the game, I didn't want to talk to

anybody," recalled McAuley. "I came into the dressing room and I was burning. [New York defenseman] Bucko McDonald came over to me and said, 'Hey, don't let it worry you. There've been a lot of goalies in this league, and none of them ever set a record.'"

The beating turned things around for the Rangers. They had been in a pattern of losing two and winning one. Now they started a remarkable streak. They failed to win their next 25 games. Needless to say, New York finished last in a dismal season. And McAuley set a lousy mark that still stands. He gave up an average of six goals a game.

According to McAuley, though, some good did come out of the Detroit disaster. After the shameful rout, he said, "Where would all those Red Wing players have been without me? I gave them the confidence they needed to become big stars."

HANK PFISTER
National 21-and-Unders Tournament ★ June 27, 1976

Hank Pfister had his ground stroke in tune, but what he really needed during one major amateur tournament was a strong swim stroke.

Before Pfister became a world-ranked tennis pro, he was a Junior Davis Cup player. In the 1976 National 21-and-Unders tourney in New York City, Hank made it all the way to the finals. But in the first game of the fifth set, he lost his serve. Hank was so mad at himself that he threw his racquet up in the air.

"I had no intention of throwing it over the fence," Pfister recalled, "but it hit the top of the fence and bounced over. The courts were situated right on the bank of the East River, and wouldn't you know, the racquet struck some rocks below and then went right into the river.

"So even though there were about 1,500 people in the stands, I halted play and went after my racquet. I went down to the edge of the water and tried to reach out for the racquet, but I missed it. The current was carrying it farther down the river, and I figured I had one more chance. I took one step into the water and went straight down. The riverbank didn't angle out into the water, so I wound up totally underwater. When I got back to the surface, I grabbed my racquet and swam back to shore.

"The East River is not exactly the cleanest river in the world, and when I returned to the court dripping wet, I had green gunk hanging all over me. The crowd went nuts and cheered and laughed. The umpire didn't know whether to default me or not. Finally he said, 'Let's play.' I had been out on the court for four hours, had blown a two-set-to-love lead, and taken a swim in the East River, so I wasn't in the best frame of mind. I

Lineswoman Dorothy Cavis-Brown takes a Wimbledon snooze.

got another racquet and finished the set—and lost the match.

"It was definitely shameful. But now as I look back on the whole thing, it sure was funny."

DOROTHY CAVIS-BROWN
Lineswoman ★ Wimbledon ★ June 22, 1964

Imagine waking up from a nice snooze. You stretch, expecting to see the light streaming in your bedroom window. Instead, you bolt up with a sick feeling in the

pit of your stomach. You realize that you're on a tennis court at Wimbledon. Worse, two players and thousands of fans are pointing and laughing at you.

That's what happened to lineswoman Dorothy Cavis-Brown. She fell asleep in the middle of the world's oldest, most dignified tennis tournament.

Dorothy was one of the most respected lineswomen in England at the time. Her job that day was to watch one of the sidelines in a match between American Clark Graebner and South African Abe Segal. Staring at the line got so downright boring that she dozed off in the final set. At first, all eyes were on the tennis action. No one noticed the prim and proper Englishwoman nodding and tilting in her chair.

Graebner, who wound up losing in straight sets, didn't realize Dorothy was asleep either. Not at first, anyway. Then Segal hit a shot wide of the line and Dorothy didn't call it "out." In fact, Dorothy didn't call it anything. Instead of 40-love, it was 40 winks. "I noticed that she was slumped over slightly, head down," Graebner recalled. "I went over and nudged her. Frankly, it was to see if she had died. Well, she bobbed her head slightly, but she didn't wake up. Eventually she did, but by then everyone had noticed her dozing. In the stands there was quite a lot of uproarious laughter, at least by British standards."

The officials at the All England Club were embarrassed. They decided Dorothy needed some time off to catch up on her sleep. She was rarely seen at the club again. Some said Dorothy was spending most of her time in the land of Nod.

The Newest Inductees

NORM McMILLAN'S INSIDE-THE-JACKET
GRAND SLAM HOMER
Aug. 26, 1929

Of all the grand slammers ever clubbed, none was more unearned than the one swatted by Norm McMillan. That's because Lady Luck had something up her sleeve.

The Chicago Cubs and the visiting Cincinnati Reds were tied 5–5 in the bottom of the eighth inning. The bases were loaded when McMillan, the Cubs' third baseman, stepped up to bat.

McMillan bounced a base hit over the third base bag. It looked like a two-run double as the ball rolled toward the Chicago bull pen. At Wrigley Field, the bull pen is located in foul territory along the left-field line. The Cubs' relief crew scattered to get out of the way as Cincy's rookie left fielder Evar Swanson raced over to where he thought the ball should be. But it was nowhere in sight.

The Chicago runners scampered around the bases while Swanson tried to find the ball. He searched over, under, and around the bull-pen bench. He still couldn't find it. By the time McMillan crossed home with a grand slam, Swanson was having fits. He needed to throw something. Cubs relief pitcher Ken Penner's warmup jacket was lying under the bench so Swanson grabbed it and hurled it to the ground in disgust. The ball rolled out of the jacket sleeve!

McMillan's cheap inside-the-jacket homer was the only grand slammer of his career. But it won the game, 9–5.

SAMMY WHITE
Catcher ★ Boston, A.L. ★ Aug. 28, 1956

Angry over an umpire's decision, Boston Red Sox catcher Sammy White tried to show him up. So he hurled the ball into deep center field. He stood proudly over his act of rebellion—for a moment. Then he realized that the ball he had thrown was still in play.

White stood stunned as the runner on first trotted around the bases and scored.

Sammy's temper flared up at Fenway Park in the top of the sixth inning with the Detroit Tigers leading Boston, 3–0. Detroit's Bill Tuttle was on second base when Red Wilson slapped an infield hit. Tuttle sped around third and dashed for home without stopping. Shortstop Milt Bolling pegged the ball to White at the plate. But umpire Frank Umont called Tuttle safe.

Sammy blew a fuse. Flinging off his mask, he charged after the ump and cursed him. Then, in a final act of public disgust, White heaved the ball into center field. This was not a wise thing to do for three reasons. No. 1, the ball was still in play. No. 2, center fielder Jimmy Piersall had trotted in to second base and was standing there with the infielders watching White's tantrum. No. 3, Umont had just ejected White from the game.

The ball was just sitting there in the outfield. So Red Wilson took off for second. Wilson rounded the bag and headed for third. Left fielder Ted Williams retrieved the ball and tossed it back into the infield.

Meanwhile, White and Bosox manager Pinky Higgins were carrying on with Umont. So Detroit's third base coach, Billy Hitchcock, waved Wilson around third. The Red Sox infielders couldn't do anything but watch Wilson score because White had his back turned to them and was out of position.

Higgins protested the game. He claimed that time was called automatically the second Umont ejected White. But the umpire declared, "White was not thrown out of the game until he threw the ball. When he threw the ball, he put it in play and we couldn't call time until the play was finished. And it didn't finish until Wilson crossed the plate."

The Red Sox lost not only the game, 6–3, but also the protest. As for White, he lost some pride and $50— from a fine levied by the league office.

MEL HALL

Outfielder ★ Cleveland, A.L. ★ March 16, 1986

Left fielder Mel Hall got so caught up in a spring training game that he hung his head—and uniform—in shame.

The Cleveland Indians were playing the Oakland A's in Phoenix. In the fourth inning, A's batter Carney Lansford hit a looping line drive over third base. Hall chased the ball into foul territory near a fence between the field and the bleachers.

Suddenly, Hall stopped dead in his tracks. He looked like he had been caught in a stop-action video replay. That's because the fence had snared the long-sleeved T-shirt under his jersey and Hall couldn't move. All he could do was watch as the ball bounced merrily away from him.

Shortstop Julio Franco raced out to retrieve the ball. When he realized that Hall was all hung up, all Franco could do was laugh. Meanwhile, Lansford circled the bases for an inside-the-park home run.

While Hall was still trying to free himself, his manager, Pat Corrales, began arguing with umpire Don Denkinger. Corrales claimed that the ball was foul. Oakland manager Jackie Moore said, "This is the first time I can remember a discussion about whether a player, rather than the ball, was in play."

After Hall unsnagged himself, teammate Joe Carter had a suggestion: "Mel needs a tear-away jersey."

RON "ROCKY" SWOBODA
Outfielder ★ New York, N.L. ★ May 23, 1965

Ron Swoboda's temper tantrum was so pitiful that he was thrown out of the game—by his own manager!

Swoboda, then a twenty-year old rookie right fielder with the New York Mets, was playing against the Cardinals in St. Louis. Despite the rainy weather, the Mets were leading 7–2 in the bottom of the ninth. But their motto was, "The game is never over until the final error." The Cardinals rallied for two runs and loaded the bases. They were down to their last out with Dal Maxvill, a .135 hitter, at the plate.

"Just then the sun popped through the clouds," recalled Swoboda. "We'd had so many rain delays that when I went out to right field for the ninth, I forgot my sunglasses. The prudent thing would have been to call time and go get them. But that would have been embarrassing to me. Of course, what happened next was much more embarrassing.

"Maxvill hit a dying quail in front of me and I lost it in the sun. The ball got by me for a three-run triple and the Cards tied the score."

The game went into extra innings and Swoboda went into the dugout cussing at himself over his misplay. Batting second in the top of the tenth, Ron was determined to make up for it. Unfortunately, all he did was repeat Maxvill's performance. Swoboda hit another dying quail to right field of all places. The only difference was that this bird was easily caught.

"We went three up and three down and I was still in a terrible state of mind," Swoboda recounted. "As I

"Rocky" Swoboda yucks it up between temper tantrums.

headed up the dugout steps to take my position in
right, I saw my batting helmet upside down on the
ground. So I jumped on it in anger. But it didn't break.
Instead, I got my foot caught in it.

"There I was out in front of the dugout, hopping on
one foot, trying to get the helmet off my spikes, when

out came [manager] Casey Stengel. He grabbed me by the shirt and kicked me in the rear and yelled, 'When you popped out to right, I didn't run into the clubhouse and throw your watch on the floor and jump on it, so I don't want you busting up the team's equipment!'

"I started to run out to right field, still trying to shake the helmet off my foot. I know I must have looked like a hundred-percent fool out there. Casey yelled at me to come back and then he threw me out of the game.

"The Cardinals went on to win in the 13th inning. It was all my fault. I was totally out of control, and Casey did the right thing when he jerked me out of the game. I went into the clubhouse and cried. It seemed like the only thing to do."

ED "WHITEY" APPLETON
Pitcher ★ Brooklyn Dodgers ★ Aug. 7, 1915

In a line of nice guys who finished last, Ed Appleton brought up the rear.

The rookie pitcher for the Brooklyn Dodgers was so polite that he did just as he was told—by the opposing manager. Even when the crafty skipper asked him to throw the game away.

Appleton was pitching in the bottom of the seventh inning against the St. Louis Cardinals when he found himself in a real jam. With the score tied 4–4, the Cards loaded the bases with two out. The pressure was building.

St. Louis manager Miller Huggins decided it was the perfect time to try to con the tense young hurler.

Coaching at third base, Huggins yelled to the mound, "Hey, Appleton! Let's see that old ball!"

Appleton had been raised to be polite and respect his elders. Apparently, he wasn't raised to be very smart. He was eager to please as important a baseball man as Miller Huggins. So Appleton turned toward the coaching box and tossed him the ball before the disbelieving Brooklyn infielders could do anything. As the ball floated through the air, Huggins stepped aside, grinning, and watched it bound toward the third base box seats. Jack Miller and Tommy Long, the runners on third and second, scampered home. The Cardinals won 6–4.

The newspapers wrote about baseball differently in those days. "Miller's face was wreathed in a smile," said an account in the *St. Louis Republic*. "Huggins, the arch perpetrator of the trick, scratched his chin and looked away from Umpire [Bill] Klem . . . Uncle Wilbert Robinson, who managed the Brooklyn outfit, seemed suddenly to have swallowed a catcher's mitt."

Because of Huggins' trick, the rules were changed. Coaches were not allowed to act in any manner to draw a throw by a fielder. But the rule change came much too late for poor Appleton. He lasted only two years in the bigs.

CHICKEN WOLF'S HOMER
Aug. 22, 1886

A player named Chicken Wolf hit a homer that could only be called a doggone shame. He needed the help of a snarling canine to beat the Cincinnati Reds with a game-winning four-bagger.

The visiting Reds had battled the Louisville Colonels to a 3–3 tie when Wolf, the Colonels' rightfielder, stepped to the plate. It was the bottom of the tenth inning, and all eyes were on Chicken Wolf, who had smacked a game-tying homer in the ninth. No eyes were on the mangy mongrel dozing at the base of the center-field fence.

That would soon change. Chicken Wolf slammed a drive to deep center field. With the crack of the bat, Reds outfielder Abner Powell took off. And so did the suddenly wide-awake dog. The mutt got to Powell before Powell got to the ball.

The dog clamped its jaws shut on Powell's pants just below the back of the knee and wouldn't let go. Chicken Wolf galloped around the bases while Powell tried to shake himself free. Finally, in desperation, Powell started hopping toward the ball, dragging the dog behind him. Chicken Wolf crossed home plate with the game-winning, inside-the-park home run before Powell broke the mutt's grip. Poor Powell—remembered a hundred years later only for dogging it in the outfield.

NEW YORK METS
Sept. 2, 1965

The New York Mets should have hired a talent agent to take their funniest fielding performance on the road. It wasn't baseball; it was slapstick comedy.

Tug McGraw watches in vain as his team blows another game.

In those days, the Mets were known as the clowns of the game. This one proved it. The Mets turned an ordinary single into a four-run, three-error play that left the crowd laughing.

The Mets were losing to the Pirates 2–1 in the bottom of the fifth inning when Pittsburgh loaded the bases with one out and Donn Clendenon at the plate. Clendenon stroked a liner through pitcher Tug McGraw's legs into center field. That's when the fun began.

Center fielder Jim Hickman came charging in, bent down, and scooped up nothing but air. The ball shot right past him and rolled to the deepest part of the outfield. The runners on second and third scored easily on the error. Clendenon and Roberto Clemente, the runner on first, tore around the bases. Hickman retrieved the ball and fired to shortstop Buddy Harrelson, the cutoff man. Harrelson tried to gun down Clemente at third, but his relay was wild and the ball bounced off the glove of leaping third baseman Charley Smith. Thankful for the back-to-back errors, Clemente darted for home.

Meanwhile, McGraw scrambled after the ball and took his shot at nailing Clemente at the plate. Instead, he nailed the on-deck circle as Tug's throw sailed over the head of catcher Greg Goossen. Clemente scored the third run of the play on the Mets' third error.

By now, Goossen had left his post at home to flag down the ball. McGraw raced to the plate to cover home where he was hoping to nab the only Pirate runner who hadn't yet scored on the play. That was Clendenon, the batter who'd hit the ball in the first place. Goossen finally picked up the ball and threw it to Tug. He whirled around to tag Clendenon, but it was too late.

The Mets had staged a real comedy—three errors and four runs on one play. At least the Mets did see one player thrown out. Unfortunately, it was McGraw.

Tug jumped up and down, cursing himself and his teammates after the "grand slam." As luck would have it, home plate umpire Al Forman was standing right next to McGraw. The ump assumed that McGraw's anger was directed at him, so Forman gave Tug the old heave-ho.

The Football
HALL OF SHAME

The Newest Inductees

CHICAGO CARDINALS VS.
DETROIT LIONS
Sept. 15, 1940

It was the worst pro football game ever played.

From an offensive point of view, it was exactly that—offensive. The Chicago Cardinals and the Detroit Lions almost bored each other to death. The game ended in a 0–0 tie that set an NFL record—for dullness. Together, the two teams gained a measly 30 yards from scrimmage. Their total yardage was 16 for the Lions and 14 for the Cardinals. A hopscotch game chalks up more yardage than that. Neither team could come up with anything that looked like an offense. They couldn't have made a point with a pencil sharpener. How boring was it? Only the lousy weather kept the 18,000 fans at Buffalo's War Memorial Stadium awake.

Shortly after the opening kickoff, a blinding, chilly rainstorm started and turned the field into a muddy quagmire fit for hog heaven. In those days, the teams played the whole game with the same ball. On top of that, there was no towel to dry it off between plays, so the football turned into a mudball.

"The mud kept getting into our faces," recalled Detroit's All-Pro center and linebacker Alex Wojciechowicz. "The worst aspect of the game was the fact that our hands kept getting burned by the lime that was formed by the combination of rain mixing with the dirt in the field. We all had to get treated for burns at some time during the game."

Neither team carried a spare set of jerseys, either. As a result, the players soon became nameless blobs. "You couldn't read any of the numbers on the uniforms and you couldn't distinguish the colors of the uniforms," said Wojciechowicz. "Everyone looked exactly the same—awful."

In spite of the terrible playing conditions, the Lions almost won the game. They completed a 26-yard pass in the third quarter. It was the only completion for either team, and accounted for Detroit's total offense. Quarterback Dwight Sloan had lobbed a wet, wobbly pass to halfback Lloyd Cardwell. The back made an amazing catch and slogged down the field until he was tackled on the one-yard line.

Strangely, Sloan didn't tighten up his offense for the expected plunge into the line. Instead, he stayed with the spread formation. It was a bad move. Taking the snap seven yards behind the line of scrimmage, Sloan was sacked twice—first for five yards, and then for seven. On third-and-goal from the 13-yard line, he heaved a desperation pass. It was intercepted.

From then on, both teams went into a prevent offense. During one stretch, they traded eight punts in a row without a single play from scrimmage.

Chicago made only two first downs all day. The Cardinals tried two passes that failed, and lost one fumble. Though they rushed for minus ten yards, the Lions made five first downs. They completed one of six passes and lost three fumbles.

The only time the soaked, bored fans got excited was after the public address announcer said, "There are only two minutes of play left." The crowd gave the announcer a standing ovation.

BILL COSBY

Alumnus ★ Temple University ★ Nov. 30, 1984

Bill Cosby—yes, *the* Bill Cosby—should have been flagged for intentional grounding.

In the middle of a college game, the superstar comedian played a major league joke. Cosby sneaked onto the field, swiped an official's flag, and buried it under the turf. When Cosby was ordered to find it, he tried, but couldn't.

Temple University

Bill Cosby goes in search of the ref's missing yellow flag.

Cosby's alma mater, Temple University, was playing the University of Toledo. He was part of the grounds crew at the Atlantic City, New Jersey, Convention Center where the nonconference clash took place. To turn the indoor arena into a football field, pieces of sod were laid over the cement floor. The sod got kicked up a lot during the action, so there were frequent delays during the game to replace it. The groundsmen, including Cosby, had to run out and tamp down the loose sod.

In the third quarter, a Toledo player ran into the Temple punter and referee Larry Glass threw his penalty flag. That was when Cosby decided to have some fun—at the ref's expense.

Decked out in a Temple sweatshirt, Cosby sneaked onto the field, took the flag, and buried it under a piece of sod. Glass gave the signal for running into the kicker, talked to the team captain, and marked off the penalty. Then he walked back to the spot where he had thrown the flag. But he couldn't find it. According to Glass, here's what happened next:

One of the players told Glass, "Cosby buried your flag under one of those pieces of sod."

Glass held up the game and marched over to Cosby on the sideline and asked, "Where's my flag?"

"Can you finish the game without it?" asked Cosby, smiling.

"No," said Glass. "I need the flag. Get it now!"

"I know right where it's at," Cosby said. But he only *thought* he knew where it was. While the players waited, he and some other groundsmen looked for it. They pulled up a dozen pieces of sod without finding the hidden flag. "Oh, well, it's under there somewhere," Cosby told Glass. "We'll find it."

"What am I supposed to do between now and the end of the game?" asked Glass. Just then another official walked over. He had brought along an extra flag, which he gave to Glass. Meanwhile, the Toledo coaches demanded that Temple be penalized for the Cosby-caused delay. The ref refused.

Temple won the game 35–6. Afterward, Cosby told Glass, "I'll see that you get the flag. We're going to take up all the sod tomorrow and I'll be there and get it. Then I'll autograph it and send it to you."

Glass claims he never did get his flag back. And he's still ticked off at Cosby. "To this day," said the ref, "I won't watch his TV show."

MIKE FREIDEL
Defensive Coach ★ Augustana (S.D.) College
Oct. 12, 1986

As defensive coordinator for Augustana College, Mike Freidel always told his players to hit each opponent hard enough to knock him silly.

Then during one memorable game, Freidel did just that—to his own head coach.

It happened during the fourth-quarter of Augustana's homecoming game with North Dakota. Freidel was standing on the sideline with his boss, head coach Jim Heinitz, when Augustana recovered a crucial fumble.

"I threw up my arms like Rocky in celebration, and my elbow caught Jim flush on the jaw," recalled Freidel. "He went out like a light. There he was, lying flat on his back, unconscious, with what looked like a smile on his face."

Players and assistant coaches crowded around the kayoed coach. Augustana quarterback Joel Nelson rushed over, too. But Nelson wasn't exactly concerned for Heinitz's welfare. "As I started to come to," the coach said, "Joel started shaking me and said, 'Wake up! Wake up! What play do you want me to run?'"

Heinitz, who was out cold for about thirty seconds, was still woozy afterward. His assistants in the press box called the plays for the rest of the game. Augustana won 19–10.

All through the next week, Heinitz nursed a sore back and a bitten tongue. But he joked about the incident. He said that one of the first things he thought about doing was firing Freidel. "Then I figured he could stay on the staff as long as I kept him up in the press box. I wanted to avoid another cheap shot."

Adding insult to injury, his own players honored Freidel as "hitter of the week." They named Heinitz as "hittee of the week."

At the next game, Freidel was allowed to stay on the sideline. But his reputation followed him. "I found myself all alone on the sidelines," he recalled. "No one would get near me during the game. Whenever a player had to talk to me, he made sure his helmet was on and his mouth guard was in."

LAMAR UNIVERSITY CARDINALS
Oct. 11, 1986

The Lamar University Cardinals were ready to kick the game-winning field goal in the closing seconds. Wisely, they let the clock wind down. But stupidly, they forgot to call timeout! Before they could attempt the kick, the final gun sounded and signaled their defeat.

Lamar made its great goof at the end of a home game against the Northeast Louisiana Indians. Late in the fourth quarter, the Indians had taken a 22–21 lead. But the Cardinals then drove 68 yards to a fourth and goal at the one-yard line. Lamar coach Ray Alborn decided to run down the clock and take a delay of game penalty. He didn't want Northeast to have time to come back after the kick. The coach also figured the five-yard penalty would help placekicker Mike Andrie because he would have a better angle from which to attempt the winning field goal.

With just three seconds left to play, the referees tossed a flag and assessed the Cardinals the delay of game penalty. Andrie then jogged onto the field and set up to boot the winner. But he never got the chance.

Under a new rule made in 1985, Northeast could choose when to have the clock restarted. It could be when the ball was snapped, or after the penalty. Naturally, the Indians took the option to restart it after the penalty. In that case, all Lamar had to do was call timeout. But the Cardinals wrongly thought that the clock didn't restart until the snap. They learned otherwise, watching in horror as time ran out.

The 22–21 defeat stretched Lamar's losing streak to

13 straight—a school record. The Cardinals were stunned. They wandered around the field after the game for about ten minutes. The Indians, meanwhile, ran off the field in no time at all.

RICK EBER
Wide Receiver ★ Shreveport Steamer ★ 1974

Rick Eber was the tackiest receiver in pro football history. He caught passes others would have dropped—because he taped thumbtacks to his fingertips!

Eber illegally sharpened his skills for the Shreveport Steamer of the short-lived World Football League. "Those WFL refs were something else," he said. "I'd catch a ball and give it back to them with scratches all over it and they never suspected a thing."

Sharing his secret with The Sports Hall of SHAME, Eber explained, "I cut the tacks down until there were just little nubs left on them. Then I taped them to my fingers and covered them with shoe polish. You can really hold onto the football that way, and yet the tacks are short enough so that you won't puncture yourself or the ball."

Eber used the thumbtacks for several games, as did some of his teammates who learned the trick from him. "One of our receivers didn't have great hands, so I showed him how to use the thumbtacks. He looked terrific. One time, right in the middle of a rainstorm, he leaped for a pass and, with those thumbtacks, caught the *tail end* of the ball as it went by him. He came back

Rick Eber shows off the thumbtacks he wore to catch passes.

to the huddle and told me, 'Man, I'm gonna wear these tacks every day!'"

During an away game against the Philadelphia Bell, Eber really stuck it to his defenders. The game was played on a muddy field in a driving rain. Of course, the ball was super slippery. But thanks to the tacks, Eber snared five receptions. Two of them were for touchdowns in the first half.

"I broke some of the tacks and wore down the others, so at halftime I put on new tacks in the locker room. The towel guy saw me do it. I didn't know he was being paid by the Bell. At the start of the third quarter, he went over to the other side and squealed on me to the Philadelphia coach, who then told an official. The ref asked to see my hands. So I showed them to him—

palms down. He just said okay and walked away. That shows you how bright the referees were in the WFL. Then he came back a few minutes later and said, 'Let me see your hands again. Only this time turn them over.' When I did, he rolled his eyes and said, 'I don't believe this!' He made me go to the sideline and take the tacks off. If the refs had bothered to check, they would have found three of my teammates guilty as well. While I was being examined, the other guys were in the huddle with their hands behind their backs, unwrapping the tacks as quickly as they could."

After Eber took his tacks off, he dropped everything that was thrown his way. He never did catch another pass the rest of the game. The Steamer lucked out, though. Eber was nailed after he had hauled in the winning touchdown.

"The refs would have found me out sooner or later," he said. "They would have said, 'Why is it that every time you catch a football and hand it back to us, it's leaking air?' "

UNIVERSITY OF VERMONT CATAMOUNTS
Oct. 9, 1971

Never in the history of college football was there a more offensive—as in stinko—series of plays than those run by the University of Vermont Catamounts.

The Catamounts were playing at home against the University of Rhode Island Rams. Vermont's goal-line offense was so weak it couldn't have scored against its own marching band.

Vermont's offense ran 11 plays inside the ten-yard line. Six of them were inside the one-yard line. Yet not a single point was made. Then their dead-head defense let Rhode Island march 99 yards, two feet, and 11½ inches to score.

The Catamounts trailed 20–16 in the fourth quarter, but had a first down on the Rhode Island nine-yard line. They picked up five yards on first down and lost five on second down. Then they threw an incomplete pass on third down. Another pass on fourth down was incomplete in the end zone. But the Rams were charged with interference. The penalty gave Vermont an automatic first-and-goal from the one-yard line.

The nickname "Catamount" is another word for cougar. But Vermont played more like pussycats. They lost a yard, gained a yard, and threw another incomplete pass. Once again, Rhode Island was flagged for interference on fourth down. Once again, Vermont had an automatic first down on the one-yard line.

The only play that seemed to work was throwing an incomplete pass. It got them an interference call and an automatic first down every time. But the Catamounts stayed on the ground for the next four plays. They gained two and a half feet on first down. On second and third, they were stacked up for no gain. Finally, their sick offense was put out of its misery. On fourth down, Vermont was stopped just an inch short of the goal line.

The few remaining Vermont fans now counted on the defense to score. After all, no defense would ever get a better chance. Rhode Island was backed up on its own one-inch line. But Vermont had just one problem. It had no defense, either.

On Rhode Island's first play after taking possession, the Rams were offside. The penalty moved the ball back half the distance to the goal. Now it was on the half-inch line. And how did the Catamounts handle this stroke of good fortune? They gave Rhode Island some breathing room, by committing a five-yard infraction. From then on, the Vermont defense crumbled as the Rams drove the length of the field in a nine-play scoring drive. The TD iced a 34–22 victory for Rhode Island.

RICKY SEEKER
Center ★ Texas A&M Aggies ★ Nov. 22, 1973

DON SHINNICK
Linebacker ★ Baltimore Colts ★ Nov. 13, 1966

War isn't the only way you can end up missing in action. Just ask Ricky Seeker and Don Shinnick. In the heat of gridiron battle, they both became invisible.

It happened to Seeker while he was playing center for the Texas A&M Aggies. He disappeared during a home game against the archrival Texas Longhorns. The Aggies were counting on their fans to give the team an extra boost. But Seeker showed his teammates that they didn't need that fabled "twelfth man." They needed an eleventh man. More to the point, they needed a center.

Late in the first half, A&M was trailing 21–7, but was threatening to score. The Aggies drove to the Texas five-yard line before a penalty pushed them back to the 20. Out of timeouts, and with only eight seconds left on the clock, A&M had time for just one more play.

A score now would do more than close the gap against the favored Longhorns. It would also lift the spirits of the underdog Aggies going into halftime.

With a record crowd of 52,973 at Kyle Field watching in suspense, A&M quarterback David Walker called a pass play. He promised his teammates, "This play is gonna work!" The psyched-up Aggies clapped their hands as they broke the huddle. Racing up to the line, they knew they could score a last-second TD.

Then they realized that something was not right. There was no center to snap the ball! In a panic, Walker looked for the missing Ricky Seeker. By the time he spotted him on the sideline, the clock had expired. The Aggies had lost a golden opportunity.

What happened to Seeker? He thought for sure the Aggies were going to try a field goal. Another center always snapped the ball on kicks, so Seeker had left the field. Unfortunately for Ricky and Texas A&M, he was wrong. Coach Emory Gellard had called for a pass. The Aggies came up short one center for the play. In the end, they came up short 29 points for the game. They lost in a 42–13 rout.

A similar blunder took place in the NFL with the Baltimore Colts, who found themselves light one man during a game against the Atlanta Falcons. Baltimore linebacker Don Shinnick was on the sidelines cheering on the offense. Suddenly, the Colts coughed up the ball on a fumble. On the next play, the Falcons ran a sweep for 15 yards. Shinnick, still on the sidelines, shouted, "Come on, let's go! Pick it up out there! Don't let 'em run like that!" Just then one of the Colt coaches pounded Shinnick on the shoulder pads and said, "Shinnick, they just ran around *your* side. You're supposed to be in the game. We're playing a man short!"

CHRIS AULT

Coach ★ University of Nevada-Reno Wolf Pack
Sept. 17, 1983

Head coach Chris Ault literally ran out on his team.

His University of Nevada-Reno Wolf Pack was playing the Fresno State Bulldogs. With 8:34 remaining in the game, Wolf Pack running back Otto Kelly broke loose and scampered 89 yards for a touchdown and a 22–21 lead.

During the run, the coach really got caught up in the excitement. He began racing down the sideline alongside Kelly. When he reached the Fresno State 20, Ault realized he had gone beyond the marked-off area of his bench. That could mean a 15-yard penalty. So Ault just kept right on running! He dashed through the end zone and up a ramp. Then he ran right out of Fresno State's Bulldog Stadium.

Ault was found hiding behind a truck by a fan who said, "Say, aren't you the coach for Reno?" The coach quickly replied, "I'm just looking for a hot-dog stand."

When Ault got back to the bench, he learned his team had been penalized. His rule-breaking run cost the Wolf Pack 15 yards on the following kickoff. It also gave Fresno State good field position, and they made the most of it. The Bulldogs went on to kick a last-second field goal that boosted them to a 24–22 victory over the Wolf Pack and Ault—who simply ran out of luck.

GENE BARTH
NFL Referee ★ Aug. 14, 1971

For his debut as an NFL referee, Gene Barth took his best shot—and hit himself in the butt.

"I started off my very first NFL game quite nervous—and quite sore," admitted Barth, now a respected veteran official.

It was just before a preseason game between the Denver Broncos and the visiting Washington Redskins. Barth was getting ready in the referees' locker room. As line judge, one of his duties was to fire the gun after each period. Barth made sure the pistol was loaded with blanks and then stuck it in his back pocket.

"It wasn't easy putting the gun in my pocket, because I was nervous, and besides, there wasn't much room in those football pants," Barth recalled. "When I started to withdraw my hand, one of my fingers accidentally pulled the trigger and I fired that gun in my pocket.

"The whole officiating crew was stunned by the loud bang. It made a heck of a noise. I was shocked, too, especially from those awful powder burns all over my rear end. I was terribly embarrassed—too embarrassed to tell the other guys that I was really hurting. I went out and officiated the game. Fortunately, in football, you don't have to sit down to officiate.

"It wasn't until I returned home that I did anything

Referee Gene Barth took his best shot—and hit himself in the butt.

about my sore rear. I had pieces of fabric and other stuff embedded in my butt, and my wife had to use a pair of tweezers to pick it all out."

Barth's tail-burning tale has been a lesson for new officials ever since. Said Barth, "The veterans tell the rookie refs, 'Nothing could be worse than what happened to Gene Barth. Imagine, shooting yourself in the rear end before your very first game ever started.'"

WICHITA STATE SHOCKERS
Sept. 20, 1986

With a huge 35–3 lead early in the third quarter, it didn't seem possible for a team to lose. But the Wichita State Shockers found a way to blow it against the Morehead State Eagles.

The Shockers suffered the worst fall-from-ahead loss in NCAA history. They stumbled and tumbled to a 36–35 defeat. It was the biggest lead ever blown in college football—32 points.

"I've been coaching for thirty years and I have never, ever, ever lost a ball game like this," lamented WSU coach Ron Chismar. "It's a disgrace."

In the second half, the Shockers made just about every mistake in the book. They made two turnovers, missed a field goal, and committed several key penalties.

The Shockers fumbled on their first possession of the third quarter. The Eagles quickly turned the turnover into a touchdown and a two-point conversion. Then Morehead State kicked a 47-yard field goal. A few plays later, Wichita State got off a sick eight-yard punt that went out of bounds on its own 29-yard line. Two plays later, Morehead State scored another TD and a PAT. The once-wide margin was cut to 35–21.

Wichita Stateenjoyed that lead until three minutes remained in the game. The Eagles had the ball, but they were on their own 20-yard line. There didn't seem to be any reason for Wichita to worry. After all, the Shockers couldn't possibly give up 15 points in three minutes. Or could they?

Morehead State quarterback Adrian Breen needed only three passes to score a touchdown. The extra-point kick was good, and with 1:54 left to play, the Shockers' 32-point lead had shrunk to just seven.

Everyone at Wichita's Cessna Stadium knew that the Eagles would try an onside kick. All the Shockers had to do was fall on the ball. Instead, they fell apart as Morehead State recovered a perfect onside kick on its own 45-yard line. WSU knew it was doomed—and played like it. The Eagles—helped by a big pass inter-ference penalty—marched 55 yards. They scored a TD on a four-yard pass with just 27 seconds left to play, cutting the margin to 35–34.

Morehead State went for the tie, but Charlie Stepp's kick was wide. The Shockers began celebrating, think-ing they had won, even though they had given up 31 points in the second half. But wait. The refs flagged Wichita State for being offside. The Eagles had one last chance.

Breen ran to the sideline and begged coach Bill Baldridge to go for the two-point conversion. "Coach," Breen said, "we've worked too hard for a tie. We deserve to win. You've got to have faith in us." Besides, the Shockers defense looked like it was waiting for something awful to happen. They didn't have to wait long. Breen took the snap from center and sprinted around end on a bootleg. He danced into the end zone untouched for the winning points.

Explaining how his team blew a 32-point lead, WSU wide receiver Broc Fewin said, "We simply gave it away. It was a team effort." For Wichita State, the record-breaking defeat was a real shocker. At least fans and players will never have to endure further shame. At the end of the season, the school's football program was shut down.

BASIC WITNESS
Atlantic City Race Track ★ Aug. 26, 1974

If the racehorse Basic Witness could talk, he'd recount a tale—or more accurately, tail—of woe.

Basic Witness was entered in the Longport Handicap stakes race at Atlantic City Race Track. Going to the starting gate, he was a 6–1 favorite. Jockey Carlos Barrera sat ready in the saddle as the back stall door was closed behind him.

Moments later, the starting gate opened with a clang. All the horses broke cleanly—except Basic Witness. He didn't go anywhere. Barrera gave him a kick and a whack, but all the horse would do was paw at the dirt. Only then did the jockey find out why his mount wouldn't move. Basic Witness had his tail stuck in the rear of the gate!

"No one, not even the old-timers, had ever seen anything like it," recalled Sam Boulmetis, the track steward at the time. "At first, we thought the horse just refused to race. Then we thought there was a tailing problem. Some horses will rear up in the starting gate, so a helper will stand in back on top of the gate and hold the horse's tail up. This is called tailing and it usually keeps the horse from rearing up.

"We figured that someone was tailing Basic Witness and forgot to let go, but the film didn't show anyone behind the horse. After talking to the starter and the jockey, we determined that somehow he got his tail caught just as they were closing the back stall door of the starting gate."

Because of what happened, Basic Witness was scratched.

"It was a funny sight," said Boulmetis. "Thank goodness he didn't break real hard or he would have lost his tail for sure."

WILLIE SHOEMAKER
Kentucky Derby ★ May 4, 1957

As one of the all-time great jockeys, Willie Shoemaker stood tall in the saddle. But one time it was during a race—and it cost him the 1957 Kentucky Derby.

The day before Willie was to ride Gallant Man in horse racing's biggest event, the colt's owner, Ralph Lowe, told the jockey, "I dreamed last night that my rider misjudged the finish line in the Derby." Shoe just laughed at the nightmare and said, "Oh, don't worry about that, Mr. Lowe. That's never going to happen to me. I've been riding too long to allow something like that."

But it happened to Shoemaker the next afternoon. Charging up on the outside after the final turn, Willie made his move. Gallant Man shot from third into the lead heading down the stretch. When his mount gal-

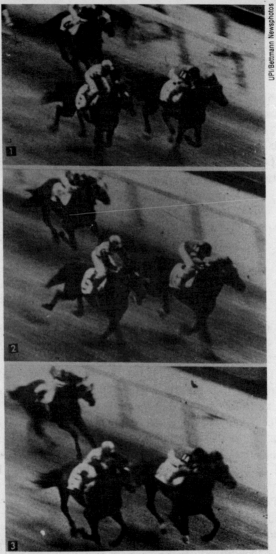

1

2

3

Willie Shoemaker (left) stands small in the saddle.

loped past the sixteenth pole, Shoe stood up in his stir-
rups, thinking he had crossed the finish line a winner.

He hadn't. All he had done was turn the colt's owner
into a prophet. Willie quickly realized he had confused
the sixteenth pole for the finish pole. He sat down
again, but the damage was done. His blunder had
slowed Gallant Man's even stride for just a second.
That's all it took to lose by a nose to 8-to-1 Iron Liege.

Recalling that shameful day, the jockey admitted in a
published account, "There can be no excuse for such a
terrible and costly moment. . . . At Churchill Downs,
the finish line is about a sixteenth of a mile farther
toward the first turn than at any other race track in this
country. I'm used to normal finish lines, and in the heat
of battling Iron Liege through the stretch, I thought the
sixteenth pole was the finish—and I stood up. Right
away I realized I had a made mistake." He said he will
always believe his blunder made the difference between winning and losing.

The Derby wasn't the only time Shoemaker blew a
major race. It happened the year before when he was
riding Swaps in the 1956 Californian at Hollywood
Park. "Swaps hadn't run in about a month and a half,"
recalled Shoe. "We wanted him to win, naturally, but
didn't want to abuse him. On this day, he looked like he
was going to win easily. At the eighth pole, I looked
around and saw I was about three or four lengths in
front, so I kind of eased up and relaxed. I got Swaps to
relax also . . . when [suddenly] I saw Porterhouse flying by us on the outside. I couldn't get Swaps to run
again quickly enough and we got beat by a head right
at the finish. It was my fault."

But it is the Derby goof that Shoemaker will always

be saddled with. Some good did come out of that embarrassing moment, though—it reined in a galloping ego. "At the time," he said, "I was beginning to believe that I was just the greatest, that I couldn't do anything wrong." At the 1957 Derby, Willie Shoemaker discovered otherwise.

PRIX DES ALPES
Steeplechase ★ Cagnes-sur-Mer, France
Dec. 22, 1968

The Prix des Alpes was supposed to be a steeplechase race, but it turned into a four-legged demolition derby.

The event, run at Cagnes-sur-Mer, near Nice in southern France, was a total disaster from the start. There wasn't a single good horse in the entire field of eleven. They all should have been in *Blazing Saddles*.

Three mounts put on the brakes at the very first water jump, and their riders flew into the pond. Guessing they'd be in a lot of trouble for such horseplay, the steeds took off.

Farther along the course, another jumper lost his rider. He tried to go through a fence instead of over it. By the halfway point, three other horses acted like rodeo broncos, as they got rid of their riders, too.

Now only four jumpers remained in the race. The steed in the lead was Gingembre, who mastered most of the obstacle course. Only a couple of furlongs from the finish, she took a wrong turn and was last seen galloping off the course. This gave Oxtail and Poisson Rouge the perfect chance to compete for first. But apparently they had no horse sense for direction either. They got lost, too, and ended up off the course, out of the running.

Now it was down to a one-horse race. The lone survivor was a filly named Fanita. All she had to do was make the last jump and trot home. However, she kept pace with the theme of the race. Fanita simply refused to jump the final hurdle. Instead, she threw her jockey, Jacques Fricotelle. He remounted, but she was annoyed, so she tossed him again. Then she took off. Fricotelle, refusing to give in to a moody mount, chased Fanita. Several yards down the course, he caught her and climbed back on.

Somehow Fricotelle convinced Fanita to take the jump. Then, just to make sure, he carefully walked her to the finish line. Fanita had won the most shameful steeplechase race ever run.

┌─────────────────────────────────┐
│   ☆   │
│   **The Auto Racing**   │
│   HALL OF SHAME   │
│   ☆   │
└─────────────────────────────────┘

BUDDY BAKER'S WILD RIDE
Smoky Mountain Raceway ★ June 6, 1968

In all of auto racing, no ride was more wild, more absurd, or more shameful than Buddy Baker's.

At the Smoky Mountain Raceway near Maryville, Tennessee, the veteran driver's Dodge blew a tire. It went out of control and smashed into a wall on the first turn. Baker was dazed and hurt, with a slight concussion and fractured ribs. He needed to get to the hospital.

"At that time, the vehicle we used as an ambulance was an old hearse," recalled Don Naman, who was then general manager of the track. "The medics put Buddy on a stretcher with wheels and loaded him into the back of the hearse. But when they closed the back door, they forgot to latch it."

You don't need much imagination to figure out what happened next. When the ambulance driver floored the gas pedal, the back door flung open. Out flew Buddy on a runaway gurney that went zipping down the track.

"There I was, strapped to this stretcher, and it was rolling clean across the track on the back straightaway

Race car driver Buddy Baker pops his cork over a wild ride.

in front of everybody," Baker recalled. What really scared him was when he saw all the other race cars. They were riding around the track under the caution flag—and were heading straight toward him. "I told myself, 'Ain't this something. Here I survive a crash head-on into a cement wall, and now I'm gonna get killed on a rolling stretcher.'"

Meanwhile, Naman was driving the pace car ahead of the field. Coming off the second turn, he spotted Baker and the speeding gurney. "When I saw Buddy rolling right toward us, I waved the other cars over as close to the wall as we could get," said Naman. "Then we all watched Buddy ride past us on that stretcher. When I looked the other way, I saw the ambulance drivers chasing after him. It was the funniest thing I've ever seen."

The medics finally caught up with Buddy and wheeled him back to the hearse. But he refused to get into the back again. "I got myself off that stretcher and squeezed into the front seat with them," said Baker. "I didn't want to get killed laying down on a stretcher.

"But, man during the ride to the hospital I kinda wished I had been knocked out. It was wild! They were running wide open, and they ran through a red light and a car pulled out in front of us. I thought, 'Oh no, here we go again!' " The hearse swerved in the nick of time to miss the car. But it skidded up on the sidewalk and plowed into some garbage cans. It made it to the hospital with a flat tire and hardly any brakes.

"I was so relieved to get to the hospital in one piece that I almost jumped out and ran in there myself," said Baker. "After I was treated and released, they offered to drive me back to the track in that hearse, but I told them, 'Never mind. I'll find another ride.' "

MYRON CAVES
Car Owner ★ Indianapolis 500 ★ May 17–25, 1969

Owner Myron Caves could have had his car in the Indianapolis 500's most desirable starting position— the pole. But his lamebrained strategy wrecked his chance of even making the field.

Back then, the rules were different. Each driver had

three chances to qualify by being one of the 33 fastest. But the pole position was decided on the first day of time trials.

Since the day was wet and blustery, the veteran drivers made a gentlemen's agreement that no one would try out.

But late that afternoon, Caves sent out his rookie driver, Jigger Sirois, to qualify. Jigger did as he was told. He hopped into his Quaker State Gerhardt-Offenhauser and headed around the slick, wet track. Winning the pole position would be easy. He just had to go four laps at a better speed than the slowest qualifier.

In his first three laps, Jigger recorded speeds of 161.783, 162.279, and 160.542 mph. They were solid times, but Caves wasn't satisfied. He wanted faster speeds. Caves waved Jigger in before he could complete his fourth lap.

The next day, Sirois went out again. This time, his speeds were 162.308, 162.660, and 162.376 mph. Caves was just as unhappy as the day before. Again, he ordered Jigger back to the pits after the third lap.

But Caves didn't know what real unhappiness was until the next day. In Sirois' final attempt to qualify, his engine broke a valve on the first lap.

What a shame. The slowest qualifier in the race was Peter Revson, who averaged 160.851. Jigger would have qualified if he'd finished just a fourth lap at 160 mph. Not only that, but Caves' car would have won the pole position. Instead, Caves' car didn't even make it into the race. And poor Jigger never got another chance to drive in the Indy 500.

But his name won't be forgotten by the racing world. The American Automobile Racing Writers and Broadcasters Association started a trophy called the Jigger Award. It's presented each May at the Indianapolis Motor Speedway. The winner is the driver who encounters the dumbest or most unlikely happening during the time trials of the Indy 500.

RICKY RUDD
Atlanta 500 ★ March 23, 1975

Ricky Rudd turned into a hit-and-run driver in his first major race. But there were no injuries—except to his pride.

"My first time on the big speedway was a little embarrassing, to say the least," confessed Rudd.

Rudd made his shameful debut during the Atlanta 500 at the Atlanta International Speedway. He was just nineteen at the time.

Ricky, who was driving a 1973 Ford Torino fastback, was on the fourth turn, when two cars tangled in front of him. "I slammed on the brakes and spun out," Rudd recalled. "I skidded down the frontstretch backward against the wall. It was my first time in an accident, and I knew I had to get out of there real fast. The crash happened on the side of the fuel filler, and I was sure the car was going to catch fire and blow up. So I unbuckled my seat belt and ran across the track and jumped over the pit wall to safety.

"A NASCAR official came over to me and said, 'What's the matter?'

"And I said, 'My car is all smashed up and it's ready to burst into flames.'

" 'No it's not,' he said. 'All you did was scrape a little

paint off your car. Now go out there and move it because it's blocking the track!'

"Shoot, all this time I thought I had destroyed it," said Rudd.

LLOYD RUBY
Indianapolis 500 ★ May 30, 1969

During a pit stop that he will always regret, 1969 Indianapolis 500 leader Lloyd Ruby became too impatient and took off. Unfortunately, what he took off was the side of his car. And that left him in the pits—in every sense of the word.

"I never felt worse in a race than I did during that one," said the veteran. Ruby is known as one of auto racing's real hard-luck drivers. Time and again, misfortune had beaten him to the Indy finish line. In 1966, he was black-flagged for an oil leak. In 1968, he led for 19 laps before a coil conked out. Two other times, he lost the rear end of his car.

But in 1969 it looked like Ruby would finally outrun his bad luck. He was driving a picture-perfect race in his Laycock-Offenhauser. He was leading on the 105th lap when he headed in to refuel.

His pit crew was using a fueling hose with a special locking device that attached to the gas-tank fitting on his car.

"I was sitting in the car, staring straight ahead, concentrating on the race, and getting ready to move out," Ruby recalled. "When the crewmen had filled one of the tanks, I thought both tanks had been refueled so I moved out. Or at least I tried."

Ruby jammed his foot on the accelerator and released the clutch. His car lurched forward only a few yards. Then he heard a sickening sound and felt an awful tug. Ruby hadn't given his crew enough time to uncouple the fuel hose. It was still attached to his car's tank fitting. He ripped out a vital section on the left side of his thin-skinned car that included the fuel tank. Gasoline spilled out onto the pavement in pit row. With it went Ruby's chances of winning.

"When I got out of the car and looked at it, I just couldn't believe it," Ruby recalled. "In fact, I had to go back and look at it again and again. What a sickening sight. Everything had been running so smoothly, and suddenly I was out of the race. I can't remember more disappointment than that day. It just seemed that the race wasn't meant for me.

"Three times I have felt like I was going to win the Indianapolis 500. Three times I have wound up with an empty feeling in my stomach. If that feeling comes from a broken heart, mine must be in a million pieces.

"I'd been racing for a long time, and this was the first and only time that my refueling got so screwed up. It was just one of those freak things. I can laugh about it now, but, boy, it sure hurt back then."

DAVID PEARSON
Rebel 500 ★ Darlington Raceway ★ April 8, 1979

It's not unusual for a stock car to take a curve on two wheels. But David Pearson tried to run a race that way.

The Silver Fox has won more than his share of races

Race car driver David Pearson fumes in his two-wheeler.

Charlotte News/Elmer Horton

by being smart. But he left his brains in the pits during the 1979 Rebel 500 at Darlington Raceway.

Midway in the race, Pearson pulled his Mercury into the pits. He was running fourth at the time. His crack pit crew decided to change all four tires on the stop. But Pearson wasn't paying attention to his pitmen. His eyes were glued on the leader and eventual winner, Darrell Waltrip. He had come in for a pit stop, too.

Pearson assumed only the tires on the car's right side were being changed. He assumed wrong. When the crew finished with the right side, they loosened the two left wheels. Suddenly, to their complete surprise, Pearson gunned the motor. Crewman Eddie Wood yelled, "Whoa!" but Pearson thought Wood was shouting "Go!"

Pearson drove off, running over the lug wrench one of the crewmen was using. Pearson's car didn't get very far. About 50 yards down pit lane, both left wheels flew off and the Mercury came to a screeching halt. The runaway wheels bounded past wide-eyed crewmen, who jumped out of their way. Crew chief Hoss Ellington barely escaped getting run over by one of them. Later he admitted, "It scared me. It almost took my head off."

Meanwhile, back in his two-wheeler, Pearson pounded on his steering wheel. He was both angry and embarrassed. "I was so intent on beating Waltrip out of the pits, I forgot about the four-tire change," Pearson explained later. "I didn't even realize the crew was on the left side of the car. Of all the things that have ever happened to me, I can't think of anything worse."

Glen Wood, for whom Pearson was driving, was steaming mad over the blunder. "We all make mistakes," said Wood, "but this was a big one."

After everyone cooled down, someone suggested that Pearson should think about "re-tiring."

The Olympic
HALL OF SHAME

OLYMPIC GAMES
Paris ★ 1900

The Olympics have withstood boycotts, terrorists, fraud—and the Games of 1900.

The 1900 Games were anything but organized, although 22 countries were represented. Many of the 1,330 athletes didn't even realize they were competing in the Olympics.

The event was treated like a sideshow for the 1900 International Exposition in Paris. The French government didn't want the Olympics to upstage its industrial exhibits. So they refused to use the word "Olympics" in the program. The Games were simply called "international championships."

The facilities were simply called awful. The track and field events were held at the Racing Club of France in the Bois de Boulogne. Being the main park in Paris, it was a terrific site—for picnicking, not running. The French refused to install a cinder track because they didn't want to ruin the grass. Runners had to race on an uneven grass field that sloped in many areas. The hurdles were built over bumpy, bush-covered ground and some were nothing more than broken telephone poles.

Discus and hammer throwers didn't even have enough room to compete. Most of their throws landed in the trees that surrounded the fields. The discus champion hurled the discus into the crowd three times. French officials, who were lukewarm about the Games at best, never even considered removing the trees.

The jumpers were ready to jump out of their skins because there were no proper pits. They were forced to dig their own—with their cleated shoes.

There were a lot of problems within the French Olympic organizing committee. As a result, there was a shortage of good officials. This created heartache and anger for several U.S. athletes, including pole vaulters, Charley Dvorak of Michigan and Bascom Johnson of New York. French officials told them that the pole vault final would be held the following day, so the two athletes went off to explore Paris. Just a few minutes later, the officials changed their minds. The finals were staged that afternoon—without Dvorak and Johnson.

The 55 American athletes were stunned by the poor planning and the low attendance. At one time, the Olympians on the field outnumbered the spectators in the stands. Even then, most of the fans were American tourists. But the Americans toughed it out, and won 17 of the 23 events.

They would have won 18, but they were cheated in the marathon. At first, it was to be run on a course from Paris to Versailles. Most of the runners had carefully studied the route. Then, at the last moment, the French officials switched to a different course and sent the runners through a maze of Parisian streets. Throughout the race, bumbling officials failed to check the runners properly and didn't keep them from going astray. Several runners went off course, accidentally or otherwise.

The American favorite was Arthur Newton, who took the lead at the midway point and was never passed. He fully expected to be the winner when he trotted to the finish line. To his shock, he was told that he had finished fifth. The officials said he was behind a Swede and three Frenchmen. The alleged winner was Michel Teato, a Parisian bakery boy. There was no doubt that Teato knew the course—and its detours— well. Perhaps too well. The Frenchman didn't look like he had run farther than a few blocks. "There wasn't a drop of mud on him or the other two Frenchmen," fumed American runner Walter Tewksbury. "Everyone else in the race was drenched with the stuff."

Teato's running was hardly Olympian in character, but then neither were some of the events. Among the "sports" in the 1900 Games were croquet, fishing, and billiards. Also on the list—believe it or not—was checkers!

MARATHON RACE
St. Louis Games ★ 1904

No Olympic marathon race was more shameful than the one run in the 1904 Games in St. Louis.

The first runner across the finish line was disqualified for hitchhiking! The next runner wasn't disqualified, but he should have been. And the runner who deserved to win ate too many green apples along the way and was defeated by cramps.

Meanwhile, another contender lost a chance for the gold because he was running from an angry dog.

It was a race that was doomed from the start. The organizers must have wanted it that way. They plotted a cruel course over seven hills on dusty roads. And they held the event on a hot, muggy 90-degree afternoon.

Only 14 of the 32 starters even made it to the finish line. Many of them choked on the dust raised by dozens of autos. The cars, carrying reporters, doctors, judges, and coaches, chugged alongside the runners.

The race took about an hour longer than the usual marathon. Three hours passed before the first runner crossed the finish line. That was Fred Lorz, of New York. Lorz was photographed with Alice Roosevelt, the daughter of President Teddy Roosevelt. Looking fresh as a daisy, he waited to receive his gold medal. Then somebody stopped the show by announcing that Lorz was a phony. Officials were told that Lorz had ridden in a car for nearly half the race. They disqualified him on the spot.

Lorz admitted to the scam. He said he was seized by cramps and quit running about nine miles out. So he hopped into a car and rode for the next 11 miles. Along the race route, he waved and joked with the other runners. Then the auto broke down about five miles from the finish line. Lorz was feeling better, so he jumped out and ran the rest of the way. When he entered the stadium, thousands of spectators rose to their feet and cheered him as he circled the track and crossed the finish line.

Lorz claimed it was just a prank. He said he had not planned to go on with the joke, but he couldn't resist the cheers of the crowd. The Amateur Athletic Union was not amused. They banned him from marathon competition for life. (However, the ban was lifted months later. Lorz went on to win the Boston Marathon the next year—without a car.)

Lorz's practical joke took some of the joy away from Tom Hicks, the real winner. (It was similar to a scene that happened 64 years later. In 1968, a hoaxer named Norbert Sudhaus stole the limelight from marathon winner Frank Shorter. Sudhaus had appeared on the track a couple of minutes before Shorter and ran a full lap before security guards hustled him away.)

About seven miles from the finish line, Hicks was exhausted and in pain. He wanted to quit, but his handlers refused to let him. They ran along with him, feeding him egg whites mixed with brandy and other painkillers which were against the rules.

Just as the fuss over Lorz was fading, Hicks staggered to the finish line in a daze. He had to be carried to a dressing room, where four doctors worked to revive him. The English-born brass worker from Cambridge, Massachusetts, accepted the gold medal. Then he promptly announced his retirement.

The runner who should have won was Felix Carvajal, a five-foot-tall Cuban mailman. Unfortunately, he lost because he listened to his stomach instead of his brain.

Carvajal's countrymen had chipped in to pay his way to St. Louis. When he got to New Orleans, he lost his money in a dice game. Broke but determined, he hitch-hiked to St. Louis, living on handouts. He was half starved and exhausted when he finally arrived at the Games. A group of American athletes immediately adopted him.

Carvajal came to the starting line wearing a long-sleeved shirt, long pants, and heavy boots. His new American friends delayed the race long enough to do some tailoring. They cut off his trousers at the knees and snipped off his shirt-sleeves. They also loaned him a pair of low-cut shoes for the marathon.

Carvajal had no real training, and knew nothing about pace or timing. Needless to say, he ran an unusual race. The little Cuban jogged tirelessly along the course. He paused to talk with bystanders along the way. He laughed and cracked jokes in his broken English. All in all, he acted like he was on the job, delivering mail.

Stronger veteran runners dropped to the ground because of the heat and dust. But the fun-loving Carvajal kept pace with the leaders. Then his empty stomach got the best of him. He was so hungry that food became more important than the race itself. First, he snatched a couple of peaches from a passing official. Then Carvajal detoured into an orchard, where he ate several green apples. Not surprisingly, he developed stomach cramps and was forced to take a long rest. Even after all that, he still came in fourth. If he had just laid off the apples, Carvajal might have won the marathon.

Another runner who could have won was a South African Zulu tribesman named Lentauw. He ran well, finishing in ninth place, and he would have done better. But Lentauw was chased nearly a mile off course by a large, angry dog.

ROGER BROUSSE
Boxing ★ Paris Games ★ 1924

Long before there was a shark named Jaws, there was an Olympic boxer who deserved the nickname.

Frenchman Roger Brousse was a twenty-three-year-old middleweight who used not only his fists and footwork, but also his teeth to fight. Whenever he got into a clinch, he'd take a bite out of his opponent!

"It was found necessary to substitute for a mere boxer a man-eating expert named Brousse, whose passion for raw meat led him to attempt to bite off portions of his opponents' anatomies," reported the *London Daily Sketch*.

In the 1924 Olympics, Brousse boxed in front of his countrymen at the Velodrome D'Hiver in Paris. In his first bout, Brousse tried to make dinner out of Argentine fighter Eduardo Gallardo. The chomp champ gnawed on his foe every chance he got, and punched and munched his way to victory. Gallardo put up a beef but officials ignored him. They didn't swallow the idea that any boxer would try to devour his opponent.

Brousse's next opponent was Harry Mallin, the defending gold medal winner from Great Britain.

"Having got his teeth into a piece of Argentine meat," wrote another boxing reporter, "Brousse decided to vary the menu by sampling some of the unroasted human beef of Old England."

Against Mallin, Brousse tried again to turn the ring into a diner. Throughout the bout, which he was clearly losing, Brousse chewed on Mallin's chest. Shamefully, Brousse was named the winner by timid judges who were afraid of the rowdy French crowd.

Mallin had never lost a fight before. After the match, he tore off his uniform top and showed the judges several sets of teeth marks on his chest. Still, the referee refused to do anything about it. But the next day, the International Boxing Association disqualified Brousse. They decided his style was just too distasteful.

BASKETBALL OFFICIALS
Munich Games ★ Sept. 10, 1972

In the worst miscarriage of justice in Olympic history, bumbling referees and a power-mad courtside official cheated the U.S. basketball team out of the gold medal it had rightfully won.

The American team had beaten the Soviet squad in regulation time. But to everyone's shock, the officials gave the Russians three chances to win. On the third—and illegal—try, the Soviets scored a last-second basket for an astounding 51–50 gold medal victory in the 1972 Games. It was the first defeat ever for an American Olympic basketball team. The USA had won all 62 games since the sport first became an Olympic event in 1936.

In the final game against the Russians, the U.S. staged a great rally and trailed 49–48. Then American Doug Collins picked up a loose ball at midcourt, drove for the basket, and was fouled with three seconds left to play. In spite of the pressure, the Illinois State senior calmly sank both free throws to give the U.S. a dramatic 50–49 lead.

But then the officials stole the victory—and the gold medal—from the Americans. They gave the Soviets three opportunities to score the winning basket.

With three seconds remaining, the Soviets inbounded the ball, but it was deflected at midcourt. A crowd rushed onto the floor, thinking the Americans had won. But referee Renato Righetto of Brazil blew his whistle. He had seen the Russian coaches surround the scorer's table, demanding a timeout. The official clock showed one second remaining.

At this point, Great Britain's Dr. R. William Jones butted in. Jones, secretary-general of the International Amateur Basketball Federation (FIBA), ordered the clock set back to three seconds. What Jones did was illegal. He had no right to make any ruling during a

The U.S. Olympic basketball team shows the agony of defeat.

game. Only the referees could do that. But Jones ruled FIBA with an iron hand, and no one dared question him.

For the second time, the Soviet team took the ball out of bounds. Modestas Paulauskas' last-ditch shot was short. The horn sounded and the American players joined the crowd at midcourt. They were joyful over their comeback and apparent victory. But their happiness was short-lived.

The clock had not been reset. Jones again used power he didn't legally have. He ordered three seconds—not one—again posted on the clock. Then he informed both coaches that the Soviet team would have one last play.

Hank Iba was the U.S. coach. He had led American teams to gold medals in 1964 and 1968. Angry, Iba started after Jones and the referees. He had to be restrained by his players before play could begin again.

The Soviet team made the most of its third chance to score. Tom McMillan, the 6-foot, 11-inch forward from Maryland tried to stop the inbound pass. He waved his arms as he had on the last two attempts. But this time the referee ordered him to back off. When he did, Soviet player Ivan Yedeshko backed up and wound up. He threw the ball the length of the court to 6-foot, 8-inch Aleksander Belov. Americans Kevin Joyce and James Forbes went up for the ball with Belov. He knocked them off balance with an obvious foul which wasn't called. Then he easily sank the ball one second before time expired. The Russians had an incredible 51–50 victory.

Chaos erupted. Iba again rushed the scorer's table. Forbes wept openly. Newsmen and irate fans flooded onto the floor. "I've never seen anything like this in all my years of basketball," Iba declared.

In the wild, closing seconds, the referees neglected to call two violations. The fouls were obvious in the game films. One showed Yedeshko stepping on the baseline when making his full-court pass to Belov. That alone would have negated the scoring play and given the ball to the Americans.

The second oversight was just as bad. The refs failed to call Belov for a violation of the three-second rule. Under international rules, that rule doesn't take effect when the clock begins. It starts as soon as the official gives the ball to the player out of bounds. The refs didn't notice that Belov was inside the three-second lane for at least five seconds.

The official result of the game was delayed because Hank Iba filed a protest. It was considered by a five-man FIBA Jury of Appeals. It was a kangaroo court. The members were from Cuba, Poland, Puerto Rico, Hungary, and Italy. The Italian and Puerto Rican representatives voted to disallow Belov's basket. But the members from the three Soviet-bloc nations—Cuba, Poland, and Hungary—naturally sided with the Russians.

The U.S. team had a vote of their own, however. They all refused their silver medals because they had been robbed of their victory.

Hank Iba was a double victim. First, his team was fleeced out of the gold medal. Then, while he was arguing with officials, Iba's wallet, containing $370, was filched. "They've even taken to picking my pockets," the coach lamented in the locker room. "What else can go wrong?"

ANTONIUS LEMBERKOVITS
Shooting ★ Los Angeles Games ★ Aug. 13, 1932

Hungarian marksman Antonius Lemberkovits was gunning for an Olympic gold medal. He would have won it too, if only he hadn't hit the bull's eye—on the wrong target.

The competition in the miniature carbine match at the 1932 Los Angeles Games was fierce. The world's best shooters were hitting tens (bull's-eyes) on the ¾-inch targets at 50 meters. Lemberkovits was also shooting flawlessly and had his sights set on a perfect 300 score.

The Hungarian's aim was straight and true. Mentally, he was steady and intense. Unfortunately, he was too intense. He was thinking about nothing but keeping his perfect streak alive. Midway in the match, he forgot to look for his target number and fired a bull's-eye on the target of the shooter next to him.

Lemberkovits realized right away what he had done and immediately notified the range officials. They confirmed that he had fired at the wrong target. He had hit a ten—but under the rules, it was a complete miss.

Lemberkovits' dream of winning a gold medal had been shot down. Between that perfect miss and another shot just off the mark, he scored a 285. Had he hit his own target, he would have finished with a 295. That would have been enough to win the gold medal.

VYACHESLAV IVANOV

Single Sculls ★ Melbourne Games ★ Nov. 26, 1956

Of all the athletes who ever won an Olympic gold medal, none messed up the presentation more shamefully than Russian sculler Vyacheslav Ivanov. He managed to lose his hard-earned medal just seconds after receiving it.

The eighteen-year-old Ivanov was competing in the single sculls on Lake Wendouree in Australia. No one expected the Soviet teenager to do very well in his first Olympics. But Ivanov made a great effort with 200 meters to go and beat out the two favorites. He crossed the finish line nearly five seconds ahead of Australian Stuart Mackenzie. He was more than nine seconds in front of third-place finisher Jack Kelly, Jr., who had won almost every major single sculls title in the world.

The gold went to Ivanov, who was happy beyond belief. He clapped his hands and shouted with joy. With the other medalists, he climbed onto a float moored to the dock where the awards ceremony was to be held right after the race.

The Boy Scouts carried the cherished medals down to the float. Avery Brundage, the president of the Olympic Federation, was there to present the medals. As he handed Ivanov the medal, the young Russian jumped up and down with glee. But in his excitement, he didn't get a good grip on the gold and accidentally dropped it. The medallion fell between two slats in the float and sank to the muddy bottom of Lake Wendouree.

Ivanov threw his hands up in grief and moaned in

Russian. Brundage tried to calm him by saying, "Never mind. I'll give you another one later." But Ivanov didn't want to wait for another one. He jumped into the water and tried to find his lost medal himself. After repeated dives into the shallow lake, the crushed Russian gave up.

The next day, nearly 300 Australian school children were recruited to search for Ivanov's medal. They scoured the underwater reeds and muddy bottom, but they never found it.

"I know Ivanov wasn't happy, but it was a big ha-ha for us," recalled John Cook, a member of the United States' eight-man rowing team who was at the awards ceremony. "There were some hard feelings against the Soviets at the time because of their invasion of Hungary. So we kept joking about how that dumb Russian beats Mackenzie and Kelly and then goes and drops his medal in the lake."

ALLEN WARREN   DAVID HUNT
Yachting ★ Montreal Games ★ July 1976

The most shameful Olympic flame in history blazed not from a torch, but from a burning boat. It was a fire deliberately set by a two-man British crew in the yachting competition.

It happened in a Tempest Class yachting race in the 1976 Olympics. Skipper Allen Warren and mate David Hunt were racing their six-year-old keelboat *Gift 'Orse* on Lake Ontario. But on the tricky course, their boat slipped farther and farther behind.

Finally, Warren and Hunt decided to give up on the

race. They also decided to give up on their poorly performing boat. The two yachtsmen took some acetone and a flare and set their boat on fire! A Canadian destroyer saw the flames and came to their rescue. But Warren just waved the ship away.

"We're quite all right," the 41-year skipper told the Navy. "We always sail like this." The destroyer returned when the smoke began to cloud the finish line. After the Britishers were picked up, the big ship put the *Gift 'Orse* out of its misery by ramming it. Down went the stricken boat as the lake waters drowned the flames.

"She went lame on us, so we decided the poor old *'Orse* should be cremated," said Warren. Back on land, it turned out, he was a funeral director. "It wasn't worth taking her all the way back home. We wanted to give her a proper Viking funeral."

Added his mate, "My skipper has style, but not that much. I tried to persuade him to burn with the ship, but he wouldn't agree."

DON GENALO
Southern California Open ★ June 11, 1983

Don Genalo was on his way to winning his third Professional Bowlers Association Tournament of the year. It was the Southern California Open, at the Gable House Lanes in Torrance, California.

But in the last frame of the final game, he got mad at himself. He had left five pins—a very difficult 4–6–7–9–10 "Greek church" split. Thinking he had blown it, Genalo just tossed his next ball without looking. It landed in the gutter.

Then he found out that he hadn't needed to make the whole split. If he had only knocked down three of the five pins, he would have won. Instead, Genalo lost 214–212.

"It was just a real inexcusable, stupid mistake on my part," Genalo admitted.

"Jimmie Pritts was my opponent in the final," recalled the third-year pro. "He was bowling really well, and I figured that if he threw a strike, I'd have to double out to win. Jimmie left a ten pin on his first shot and then picked it up for a spare. But I still had it locked in my head that I needed a double. I even checked the score sheet, but I added wrong.

"I threw a strike and the crowd cheered. I concentrated on my next shot, thinking I needed that second strike to win. But I made an absolutely atrocious shot and left the 'Greek church' split and I thought I had lost. I figured the next roll didn't mean a thing, so I just threw the ball down there and it landed in the gutter. I told myself that it was no big deal. Little did I know how big a deal it really was.

"I was getting ready to congratulate Jimmie when somebody said, 'What a shame to have lost by just two pins like that.' When I found out I had added the score wrong, I wanted to bounce off the walls. I was ready to blow up the building with me in it."

It's too bad Genalo didn't realize he was only two pins behind. He would easily have picked up three pins on his next roll. He also would have picked up another $5,500. That was the difference in prize money between first and second place.

"It hurts to talk about it, but there's no way I can pretend it didn't happen, especially when millions of people saw it," he said. "You see, ABC was televising the finals nationally. It was all so stupid and embarrassing."

RICHARD CAPLETTE
Sept. 7, 1971

No one ever rolled a more terrible game in league competition than Richard Caplette of Danielson, Connecticut. It was a night no one at the Friendly Bowl in nearby Brooklyn will ever forget.

Caplette owned a decent 170 average—until that night. Then he set the American Bowling Congress record for the lowest score in league play. He bowled an incredible score of 3! On top of that, he threw 19 gutter balls—the most ever in a single game.

If the pins were as big as oak trees, it wouldn't have helped. Caplette simply couldn't hit them.

"No matter what I tried, I just couldn't keep the ball on the alley," recalled Caplette. "The biggest mistake I made that night was showing up at the bowling alley."

It was the opener of the new bowling season, and Caplette was rolling for the VFW team at the Friendly Bowl. He felt good and hoped to shoot a 200 game. But at the end of the evening, he was 197 pins short.

Caplette's first clue that this would not be his night came early. He knocked down only three pins on his first ball. He rolled his second ball in the gutter. He muttered and cursed. But he probably would have cheered if he'd known what lay ahead. That turned out to be his only scoring frame all night!

"I couldn't stop throwing gutter balls," he said. "I kept doing it frame after frame. Our scores were posted overhead, and that didn't help, especially since our team bowled in a lane right next to the women's league. After each gutter ball, I'd sit down and a different woman would come over and say, 'Can I help you?' That was bad enough. But then about the seventh frame, the president of our league hollered over to our team captain, 'Hey, Duke. Who do you have on your team tonight? A blind bowler?' I was ready to give up then, but I went ahead and finished.

"I was really trying my best, too. It was just that the

harder I tried, the worse I got. I never saw anything like it in my life."

Neither had anyone else. Of the 20 balls he rolled, 19 in a row were gutter balls.

Caplette still lives in the area, only two miles away from the Friendly Bowl. But he says he has never set foot in the place again. He even worked on the roof of the bowling alley one time but wouldn't go inside. "I just never went back," he admitted. "I completely gave up bowling after that. I never threw another ball. I was too embarrassed to show my face around an alley again."

PALMER FALLGREN
Cougar Open ★ March 20, 1971

The wildest ball ever thrown in a pro tournament wasn't a gutter ball. It was a *ceiling* ball.

It was thrown by Palmer Fallgren, during the Cougar Open at the Madison Square Garden Bowling Center. He was then a nineteen-year-old bowler in his second year on the pro tour.

"I've never had a more embarrassing moment," said Fallgren. "People still come up to me on the tour and ask if it's really true."

It happened in the eighth frame. The temperamental young bowler had left a 4–6 split. "I was so ticked off, that I didn't even wait for my ball to get back," Fallgren recalled. "I had another ball, so I just grabbed that instead, stared at the split, and then tried to throw the ball as hard as I could."

Palmer Fallgren is the only professional bowler to hit the ceiling.

In his hurry and fury, Fallgren forgot something. He had placed tape in the finger holes of his spare ball before the tourney. When he tried to release the ball on his follow-through, it stuck to his fingers. Instead of rolling the ball straight *down* the alley, Fallgren launched it straight *up*.

The 6-foot, 1-inch, 170-pound bowler threw his 16-pound ball with a lot of force. It smashed into the 15-foot-high ceiling. Then it plunged back down to the alley with a thundering bang and landed about ten feet in front of the foul line. Finally, it rolled down the lane—and knocked down the four pin!

"I went into total shock," said Fallgren. "It was so embarrassing, I didn't know what to do or what to say. When the ball hit the floor, it sounded like a cannonball, and the bowlers on all the other lanes just stopped in their tracks. I was frozen, too, just staring at the ceiling. I couldn't believe what I had done."

Although the four pin was toppled, the rules of bowling ruled out the knockdown. Fallgren was fined $100 for a "shot unbecoming a professional." However, even after all these years, he has yet to pay it.

Fallgren's ball not only made an impression on his fellow bowlers, it left its mark on the ceiling and the alley as well.

"He put a dent in the ceiling, and it's still there today," said Tom Robally, director of the bowling center. "He also dented the lane and we had to put down new wood.

"It could have been a lot worse. When Fallgren's ball hit the ceiling, it missed a sprinkler head by just three inches. Our building engineer told me that if the ball had struck the sprinkler head, we would have been flooded out."

FRAN WOLF
Dayton Classic ★ July 20, 1976

One of the worst fears bowlers have is that the ball will fly off behind them on the backswing. Third-year women's pro Fran Wolf realized this fear in one tournament. Not once, not twice, but four times.

"It's a memory that will stay with me forever," laughed Fran, now tournament director for the Ladies Professional Bowling Tour. "I lost my ball on my practice throw in each of the four rounds of the Dayton Classic.

"The first time I did it, the ball flew out of my hand behind me and crashed with a loud bang that silenced the whole place. That was embarrassing, but it got worse. In the second round, I lost my ball on the backswing again. I had hoped no one saw me, but naturally everyone had. I didn't know what to do, so I kicked my ball back toward the settee [sitting area].

"When I got up for my practice ball in the third round, I just knew it was going to happen again, so I marched up there and told myself, 'Well, let's get this over with.' Sure enough, the ball flew out of my hand on the backswing."

For the fourth round, Fran was in the finals. As a result, she was in the spotlight more than ever. She was hoping that everyone had forgotten about her wild practice throws. They hadn't. As Fran walked up to the lane, she glanced back. There, standing on the settees seeking safety, were her competitors. Faced with such a show of no confidence, Fran knew she was doomed. For the fourth time in a row, she lost her grip. Her practice ball sailed behind her, landing on the wood with a thwack. "When I turned around, everyone was applauding," she recalled. "It was the biggest applause I got during the whole tournament."

At least Fran didn't fling the most shameful practice ball. That dishonor goes to ten-time national tournament winner Vesma Grinfelds. Vesma was in the 1975 Women's International Bowling Congress tourney in

Las Vegas. She wanted to get off to a good start by firing a practice strike. She did, too. But not at the pins. Vesma lost control of her ball on the backswing. It flew out of her hand backward and crashed right into the settee!

"I casually went over to the settee," recalled Vesma, "and calmly picked up my ball and said, 'Well, that's my practice throw.'"

MARK BAKER
Miami Miller Lite Tournament ★ Feb. 4, 1984

Pro bowler Mark Baker suffered the most embarrassing split ever in a tournament—when the seat of his pants ripped open!

That day, the third-year pro revealed a new side of himself during the Miami Miller Lite tourney at Don Carter Lanes.

"I needed to get a strike in the tenth frame to beat my opponent, so I was psyched," Baker recalled. "I put something extra in my throw and I went down to one knee on the follow-through. Then I heard my pants rip.

"I didn't think much of it because I got my strike and I was really pumped up. But the crowd—it was standing room only—let me know immediately. I reached behind me and discovered a huge hole in the seat of my pants. Being from California, I wasn't a big believer in underwear, so my bare butt was hanging out for all to see."

The red-faced Baker excused himself fast. He pulled his bowling shirt out so the tail would cover up his torn pants. Then he walked through the giggling crowd to the locker room to change. "I was never so embarrassed," he recalled, "especially when everyone gave me a standing ovation."

After he changed pants, Baker just wanted to put the matter behind him. He returned to finish the tenth frame and barely beat out his opponent.

"The next day, everyone started calling me 'Moon.' I appeared on a televised tournament, and the sportscaster told the TV audience what had happened to me and my pants. The following week, I received 17 pairs of underwear in the mail from various women across the country."

JOSEPH "ACE" FALU
Junior Middleweight ★ New York ★ Feb. 26, 1962

Ace Falu achieved boxing infamy in only 14 seconds.

Falu, a twenty-two-year-old amateur, had fought in New York City's Spanish Golden Gloves. Then he decided to turn pro. But Ace had no big dreams about being a contender. He just wanted to make enough money to open a small grocery store.

His pro debut was at the old St. Nicholas Arena in Manhattan where Ace went up against Norman Cassaberry, a junior middleweight. Cassaberry had only a few pro wins under his belt. Ace was pumped up for the bout, and eager to throw his best punches. He was also ready to take his opponent's best shots. Or so he thought.

When the bell rang for the first round, Ace showed his Golden Gloves sportsmanship. He came out with his hands stretched out in front of him. The idea was to touch gloves with Cassaberry. But this was a fight, not a social. And Cassaberry had come to fight. He threw a left followed by a powerful right to Falu's chin. Ace hit the canvas seven seconds into the round. By the count of seven, Ace had bravely staggered to his feet. But referee George Coye could see Falu was too dazed to continue and he halted the bout.

Cassaberry's punches knocked out any further boxing plans for Ace. He decided then and there to quit for good. But at least he left the ring with a record. Falu had the shortest pro career in the history of prize fighting. Fourteen seconds.

JITTERBUG SMITH

Lightweight ★ New Orleans ★ Sept. 8, 1958

Jitterbug Smith kayoed his opponent—yet still managed to get *himself* counted out.

Jitterbug was pounding the daylights out of Ralph Espinia in New Orleans in the first two rounds of a lightweight bout. Jitterbug knew he had the fight won. But in the third round he toyed with his outclassed foe for another minute. Then he sent a crushing right to the jaw that turned out Espinia's lights. The loser toppled to the canvas.

Jitterbug smiled, figuring he had won the fight. All he had to do was go to a neutral corner and wait as referee Pete Giarusso counted out the fallen Espinia. But Jitterbug didn't do that. One of Espinia's weak punches must have knocked the smarts out of him because Jitterbug foolishly sat down in the ring and waited for the official count.

Giarusso counted ten over Espinia—but at the same time, counted ten over Jitterbug. Since the relaxing boxer wasn't on his feet, he was considered kayoed, too.

When the crowd stopped laughing over the rare double knockout, Jitterbug took one more swing. This one was aimed at the boxing rules. "This is too much!" declared Jitterbug. Then he announced he was retiring from the ring.

JACK WELSH
Referee ★ World Lightweight Championship
July 4, 1912

Referee Jack Welsh dealt boxing the most outrageous, lowest blow in the history of the sport by turning a world lightweight championship bout into a sham.

It happened in the 13th round of a fierce 1912 title fight between champ Ad Wolgast and challenger Joe Rivers. Wolgast and Rivers were trading punches evenly. Their faces were puffed and cut. Near the end of the round, Wolgast sent a right to Rivers' body. He followed with a wicked left—below the belt. At the exact same moment, Rivers landed an equally powerful blow to Wolgast's jaw.

Rivers crashed to the floor and Wolgast fell on top of him. Both men groaned in agony. Wolgast struggled to a sitting position, but he was too dazed to stand. Meanwhile, Rivers was sprawled full length on the canvas. His frantic cornermen were screaming bloody foul.

Welsh was faced with a truly unusual double knockdown. For several seconds, he just stared at the fallen fighters, wondering if one of them would get up. When neither one did, he decided to take matters into his own hands. What he did shocked the 11,000 fans at the Vernon Arena near Los Angeles. It also made them

Referee Jack Welsh is about to commit ring robbery.

furious. With his left hand, Welsh lifted the punch-drunk champ to his feet. With his right hand, the ref counted out the laid-out challenger. As if that weren't a raw enough deal, Welsh shortchanged Rivers on the count. He finished it a split second after the bell ended the round.

Timekeeper Al Holder shouted that he had rung the gong but Welsh ignored him. Rivers, his face twisted in pain, struggled to his feet without help. He squared away, ready to renew the battle. But Welsh waved him to his corner and declared Wolgast was still champion. Wolgast was still too dizzy to realize that he had won. He tottered around the ring until he fainted. Then he was carried back to his dressing room.

The arena turned into a madhouse. Rivers' cornermen surrounded Welsh and screamed in protest. Irate fans stormed the ring, shouting, "Robbery! Robbery!" Welsh tried to escape, but boxing promoter and attorney Earl Rogers stopped him. "It's the most gigantic wholesale swindle ever!" shouted Rogers. There was enough swearing and yelling going on to cause a cauliflower ear. Welsh somehow sneaked through the crowd and dashed out of the arena.

"It was the worst case of robbery in the history of the American ring," declared Rivers' manager, Joe Levy. "Never before have I seen a referee pick up a man and then give him the decision. The foul blow struck by Wolgast was seen by every man near ringside." Rivers backed up his claim of a low blow. In his dressing room, he showed newsmen his dented aluminum protective cup.

Later, Welsh defended his actions. He said he had made a difficult judgment call. The truth is, the ref did some fancy footwork. He toyed with the rules and gave a break to one of his closest friends. That happened to be none other than Ad Wolgast.

MUHAMMAD ALI
World Heavyweight Champion ★ Tokyo
June 26, 1976

Muhammad Ali's fighting motto was, "Float like a butterfly, sting like a bee." But in a shameful ring performance not worthy of a champion, Ali did nothing but float like a rock, sting like a moth.

For $6 million, the world's most popular, wealthiest heavyweight champion accepted an absurd challenge. He agreed to meet Japanese wrestler Kanji Antonio

Inoki in a 15-round bout in Tokyo. The promoters hyped the match as "The War of the Worlds." But Ali turned it into the bore of the universe.

It was, in fact, the dullest sporting event ever televised. For millions of fans who watched it on closed-circuit TV, it was a rip-off.

They saw Ali throw only six punches in the entire fight. That's a million bucks a punch. He landed only two harmless jabs. Meanwhile, Inoki wasn't much better. He scooted around the ring on his back like a belly-up crab and kept kicking the champ in the leg. He was trying to down Ali without getting his chin in range of Ali's reach.

Inoki, nicknamed "Pelican" because he had such a huge jaw, kicked Ali in the leg about sixty times. The champ's shin was bloodied and the back of his leg was bruised. Ali's corner worked on the leg early, applying ice bags and Vaseline. If the injury had gotten worse, it could have been a first—the first bout ever stopped because of a leg cut.

For his part, Ali clowned around and stuck his tongue out at Inoki. He gestured to the wrestler to stand up and punch with him. But Ali always managed to stay close to the ropes. That's because there were special rules for this so-called fight. Under them, Ali could stop the action—as if there were any—by grabbing the ropes.

So Inoki would try to kick Ali's legs out from under him. The champ would move to a corner and lift himself onto the ropes. Often during the match, they motioned to each other to come closer. At times, Ali danced a hula, patted Inoki's backside, and mocked him.

The "fight" between the thirty-four-year-old boxer and the thirty-three-year-old son of a Japanese farmer ended in a draw. No one was satisfied. That went double for the 14,000 fans at the Japan Martial Arts Hall. Many of them tossed trash into the ring at the end of the last round.

The Ali-Inoki comedy was supposed to settle once and for all that age-old question: "Who would win a match between a wrestler and a boxer?" One question was answered. We know who would lose. The fans.

RALPH WALTON
Welterweight ★ Lewiston, Maine ★ Sept. 23, 1946

It was bad enough getting knocked out in the first round, but Ralph Walton added insult to his own injury by setting a record for the quickest KO in boxing—ten and a half seconds!

Walton, a 142-pound welterweight from Montreal, was in his corner with his handlers. He was getting last-minute instructions before his fight with local boxer Al "Shiner" Couture. The bout, a scheduled ten-rounder, was the main event on the card at the City Hall auditorium in Lewiston, Maine.

Walton, who had a three-pound advantage over Couture, was eager to box. But he wasn't nearly as eager as his opponent. At least a second or two before the bell, Couture dashed across the ring.

Neither Walton nor his handlers noticed him. One of Walton's seconds was standing outside the ropes on the apron adjusting the boxer's mouthpiece when the bell rang.

Walton, who had his back to the ring, took his hands off the ropes and turned around. He expected to see Couture coming out of the opposite corner. To his shock, he found himself toe to toe with his opponent. Before Walton could react, Couture threw a powerful punch to the solar plexus. Walton went down in a heap, and referee Tom Breen counted him out. The fight ended a record ten and a half seconds after it began. Asked later if Couture was a good fighter, Walton reportedly said, "I don't know. I wasn't in the ring long enough to find out."

HENRY WALLITSCH
Heavyweight ★ Long Island ★ Sept. 12, 1959

Henry Wallitsch was knocked out by his own worst enemy—himself!

Wallitsch, of New York, was a free-swinging 189-pound heavyweight. He was seeking revenge on his opponent, 175-pound Bartolo Soni of the Dominican Republic. Six weeks earlier, Soni had scored a split decision over Wallitsch.

A crowd of 1,500 was on hand for the scheduled ten-round rematch at the Island Garden Arena in Long Island City, N.Y.. Early in the bout, the fighters traded a flurry of wild punches. Unfortunately, neither boxer landed any good ones.

In the third round, Walitsch flailed away, but still failed to connect. He moved in closer for some short, quick jabs. He ended up in a clinch. As he broke free, Wallitsch wound up for a haymaker and hit nothing but air.

The force of the missed punch made Wallitsch lose his balance and he pitched through the ropes head first. His chin slammed on the apron of the ring, and Wallitsch was knocked unconscious. The referee counted him out at 2:58 of the third round.

Soni never landed a punch in the round. But the record books show that he kayoed Wallitsch. In truth, however, it was Wallitsch who knocked out Wallitsch.

MIKE DECOSMO VS. LAURIE BUXTON
Welterweights ★ Newark, N.J. ★ May 18, 1948

For ten rounds, welterweights Mike DeCosmo and Laurie Buxton threw a flurry of punches, but neither could deck the other. Nevertheless, each recorded a KO—they knocked out the referee!

Fans at the Meadowbrook Bowl in Newark, N.J., were treated to a close fight. DeCosmo, a local fighter, was favored over Buxton, an Englishman. As the last few seconds ticked off, the boxers finished with a flurry, standing toe to toe and belting away at each other. They were fighting so fiercely that they failed to hear the final bell.

Referee Joe Walker stepped between the two flailing boxers and tried to separate them. Instead, they separated him—from his senses. DeCosmo and Buxton both walloped him on the chin at the same time. Walker fell flat on his back, knocked out cold.

It took a minute and a few whiffs of ammonia to revive the ref. Walker's brother Mickey was a middleweight and welterweight champ. That night, Walker showed why he could never follow in Mickey's foot-

Referee Joe Walker takes the count after getting kayoed.

steps. He couldn't take a punch—or in this case, two punches.

Walker staggered to his feet, wincing in pain. Through his sore chin, torn mouth, and chipped tooth he gave Buxton the decision. Angered DeCosmo fans then shouted that Walker should have stayed down for the count.

LANE LOHR
Pole Vaulter ★ University of Illinois ★ June 5, 1985

A funny thing happened to pole vaulter Lane Lohr on his way over the crossbar—he lost his track shorts.

It happened in the preliminaries of the 1985 NCAA meet in Austin, Texas. Lohr, a junior at the University of Illinois, had just cleared the bar at 17 feet, 2 inches. Suddenly, a gust of wind blew his pole underneath him. As he began to fall, the pole rode up his thigh, slid inside his track shorts and ripped them right off! Lohr landed in the pit wearing only his jockstrap.

"I was lying there in the pit, and the first thing I did was look up and see that the bar was still there," Lohr recalled. "The second thing I did was look down and see that all I had on was my jockstrap. My track shorts were lying beside me, ripped in half."

The crowd was hushed at first, as if no one could believe their eyes. After a few seconds, the reality set in, and the stadium rocked with laughter.

"I didn't know what to do," Lohr said. "Just then an official came running over and brought me a towel. I wrapped it around myself and jumped up and waved to the crowd. Then I went back down the runway because

I had to make another jump. I was so into the competition that I would have jumped in my jockstrap if they had let me.

"But a friend of mine who pole-vaulted for Baylor came out of the crowd and offered me his shorts. There's an NCAA rule that you must wear your team uniform. However, a track official told me that I had been granted a special exemption. So right out there in the middle of the field, my friend took off his shorts and gave them to me in exchange for my sweat pants."

Lohr placed sixth in the finals with a vault of 18 feet. It was good enough to make him an All-American. Even so, he was the butt of jokes for weeks afterward.

JEFF WOODARD
High Jumper ★ University of Alabama ★ April 24, 1981

Jeff Woodard confused the high jump in a track meet with the high dive in a swim meet.

Woodard was then the NCAA indoor American record holder in the high jump. He was competing for the University of Alabama at the Invitational Relays in Walnut, California, when he made his biggest—and most embarrassing—splash ever.

"When I arrived for the meet, I felt fantastic," recalled Woodard. "It was one of those days when just everything was clicking. I felt fast and strong." His mind was totally focused on jumping. Too focused, it turned out. When he checked out the high-jump pit area, Woodard missed something. He hardly noticed that it butted up against the water jump for the steeple race.

"At the time, I was at the top of my game and I felt

that I could break a record at the meet," he said. Woodard had a feeling it would be an unforgettable day. It was—but not in any way he could have imagined.

"The bar was at seven feet, one and three-fourths inches, and I was psyched. On the approach, I went flying. I got one of those once-in-a-lifetime plants and cleared the bar with plenty to spare."

Woodard launched himself with great force. So great that when he landed, he hit the back edge of the pit. Then he rolled over—right into the three feet of water in the steeple jump.

"I couldn't believe it," he recalled. "All of a sudden, I was looking up from the bottom of the pit and seeing those ripples on the surface. I told myself, 'Dang, I'm underwater!' I came out of the pit and shook off the water. That's when I realized that everyone in the stands and on the field was laughing at me."

Because of this incident, Woodard became the only high jumper ever to need a snorkel, fins, and mask to clear the bar.

OKLAHOMA CHRISTIAN COLLEGE'S OUTDOOR TRACK
1960s—present

The fortunes of athletes competing on Oklahoma Christian College's outdoor track have gone with the wind—for real.

It's known as the country's windiest and most wicked college track. Athletes actually get blown away there. Gusts have shoved runners out of their lanes. Sprinters have been slowed to a crawl. Pole vaulters have stalled in midflight.

OCC happens to sit on a hill overlooking Oklahoma City, the windiest city in America during spring. And spring happens to be the height of the outdoor track season. "The wind is so strong around here at that time of year that it can blow you right down and cause you fits," said track coach Randy Heath.

Pole vaulter Jeff Bennett learned all about ill winds during his track days at OCC from 1966–70. "The runway only went one way—into the wind," recalled the five-time All-American and fourth-place finisher in the 1972 Olympic decathlon. "I'd run down the runway, go up, and at about 15 feet, a twenty-mile-per-hour wind would catch me. I'd start to teeter-totter and then go backward. I'd fall back on the runway, land on my feet, and roll into a back somersault to soften the impact."

Pole vaulters haven't been the only ones stopped in midair by big blows. The wind plays havoc with the long jumpers, too. Strong gusts sweeping down the plain push slightly built milers and sprinters right out of their lanes. The quarter-milers also have cast their fate to the wind—and lost. On most tracks, the gut-it-out area in the 440 is the last 100 yards. At OCC, it starts at the second curve—the windiest spot on the windiest track. Heading full tilt into a gust is like running into an invisible wall.

"The wind has also scraped most of the cinder right off our track," said Coach Heath. "We're almost down to the bedrock now."

There hasn't been a varsity meet held at OCC since March 9, 1985. Why? The answer, my friend, is blowin' in the wind.

The High School Sports
HALL OF SHAME

HOMER (ILLINOIS) HIGH VS.
GEORGETOWN (ILLINOIS) HIGH
Basketball ★ March 6, 1930

In the most shameful high school basketball game ever played, Georgetown defeated Homer, 1–0.

The 400 fans would have relished a game decided by only a single point. But not one that *tallied* only a single point. Maybe the spectators should have been Eskimos. That way, they could have enjoyed the deep-freeze tactics. The way Georgetown froze the ball, the game might as well have been played at the North Pole. But it was in Westville, Illinois, where this contest set a record scoring low.

Georgetown guard Mike Spasavich was the game's high—and only—scorer. He sank a free throw early in the first period. After Homer missed a shot, Georgetown grabbed the rebound. Then they sat on the lead—in the truest sense of the word. The team simply made no further effort to score. Homer didn't help matters any when it played along with the stall.

Georgetown held the ball through the second, third, and most of the fourth periods. Its two guards sat on

127

the floor and rolled the ball back and forth to each other. Their teammates talked among themselves and chatted with the spectators. The players made dates, and did everything but play basketball.

Meanwhile, Homer's coach, Merle Ririe, ordered his players to their end of the court where they sat on the floor. The officials were so bored they went into the bleachers and read the newspaper.

Coach Ririe didn't rouse his players until there were only three minutes left. Then he woke them up and ordered them to break up the stall. But by then it was too late. Even if Homer had scored, most of the fans would have missed it. They had all dozed off.

EARNIE SEILER

Football Coach ★ Miami (Florida) High
Nov. 22, 1924

Football coach Earnie Seiler never tried to break the rules. He just tried to stre-e-e-tch them.

The sneakiest play he ever cooked up came during the 1924 season. At the time, he was coaching at Miami High. He took advantage of the team's unique football field which had a palm tree standing on the 20-yard line, 15 yards in from the sideline.

The tree couldn't be cut down because of an agreement. Florida East Coast Railroad had donated the property to Miami High, but the school had to promise never to remove a single coconut palm. And there were a lot of them. Somehow, Seiler laid out a gridiron among the many palms, leaving only that single tree growing in the field of play.

He waited for the season's biggest game to spring his trick play against Palm Beach High. On the kickoff, it looked like Miami had only ten men on the field. But the eleventh player, speedy halfback Ray Carter, was hiding behind the palm tree. The kickoff went to star runner Warner Mizell on the ten-yard line. He headed upfield to the palm tree. As he ran by, he handed the ball off to Carter. In the same motion, Mizell whipped off his leather helmet and threw it to the ground several yards away from the tree. His teammates yelled, "Fumble!" and dove on the helmet. Suckered, the Palm Beach players leaped into the pile-up.

Meanwhile, Carter stayed hidden behind the tree as the opposing team ran by. He was supposed to count to five and then come out, running like mad. On the sideline, Seiler was counting to himself. When he reached five, Carter still hadn't come out. "Gawdamighty, he can't count!" the coach shouted. But just then, Carter peeked out from behind the palm tree. Seeing that nobody noticed him, he scampered downfield 80 yards for a touchdown.

The Palm Beach coach charged across the field. Right behind him were dozens of Palm Beach fans. "I protest! I protest!" he screamed in rage. "It's against the rules."

Seiler smiled and spoke in a polite, calm voice. He said, "Show me in the rule book where it says you can't have a palm tree on the football field." The touchdown stood.

Seiler's creative coaching sometimes backfired. He used visual aids to help quarterback Cedric "Froggy" Buchanan call the right plays. Seiler lined up three buckets on the sideline at midfield. If the coach tipped pail No. 1, it was the signal to run. Pail No. 2 meant pass, and pail No. 3 signified punt. In one game, his team had driven to their opponent's 18-yard line. Seiler wanted Froggy to pass, but he knocked over the third pail by mistake. Froggy stared at his coach, puzzled. Then he did as he was told. He punted the ball out of the end zone. It landed in the second-floor window of the building across the street.

ED MYERS
Catcher ★ Fredonia (Arizona) High ★ April 25, 1981

Of all the scams ever run in high school baseball games, none was funnier or sneakier than the potato trick.

It was pulled off by Ed Myers, catcher for Fredonia (Arizona) High. He learned it from his coach, Clint Long, who swore it had happened once in the minors.

Fredonia was getting ready for a game against Ash Fork (Arizona) High. Myers bought a potato the size of a baseball for 22 cents and stuffed the spud in his pocket. Then he took the field in the bottom of the first inning.

"We were already ahead 7–0 and I thought that now was as good a time as any to try the trick," recalled Myers. "So we walked their star hitter, Bill Robertson, and let him steal second and third. We got him cocky, and he took a big lead off third. As soon as I caught the next pitch, I whipped out the potato and deliberately fired it over the third baseman's head."

Robertson saw what looked like the ball sailing down the left-field line. So he trotted toward home for what looked like a certain run. Myers met him about a third of the way up the line and tagged Robertson out with the ball. "Boy, was he surprised!" said Myers.

"The potato shattered on impact and our left fielder picked up the pieces and tried to eat all the evidence. I never thought the play could work so well. Our whole team just cracked up."

Not everyone was laughing. A stunned Robertson demanded, "Where'd you get that ball?" The home plate umpire scratched his head and said, "Something's wrong here." Ash Fork coach Lynn Painter finally figured out that his team had been duped and protested the "this-spud's-for-you" trick play. But Coach Clint Long stumped the huddled umpires. Gloating, he asked, "Is there anything in the rule book that says you can't throw a potato into left field?" To keep the peace, Long finally gave in. He let the home plate umpire reverse the call so Robertson could score.

Fredonia won the game 18–7. Afterward, Ash Fork fans had a little surprise of their own for the winners. They splattered the Fredonia bus with bananas.

The great potato scam left some others fried as well. The Arizona Interscholastic Association put the whole team on probation. "The officials wanted to put a stop to this sort of trickery right away," said Myers. "They had visions of catchers lugging gunny sacks full of potatoes, and of mashed potatoes covering the field."

WAVERLY (OHIO) HIGH BASKETBALL TEAM
Feb. 19, 1982

In the worst start ever in high school basketball, the Waverly (Ohio) Tigers trailed 7–0—before they even got the chance to touch the ball!

"I suppose I have to take the blame for this," recalled Tom Monroe, a Waverly teacher. He acted as the official scorekeeper for the game with the visiting Athens (Ohio) High Bulldogs. "Gabby Smith, our coach at Waverly, had a superstition that only he could put the names and numbers in the official score book. Somehow, when he entered the names of his players, he put in the numbers of their away uniforms, which are odd numbers, rather than the even numbers of their home uniforms. I didn't bother to check before the game because our players were still wearing their warmups.

"When the game was about to begin, the scorer for Athens noticed that the uniform numbers were wrong and informed the referee. By then, it was too late for us to do anything about it."

Following the rules, the ref assessed the technical fouls before play began. Each of the Waverly starters got a "T" for wearing the wrong numbers. Athens' star shooter, Steve Bruning, made all five of the resulting free throws. Because of the technicals, there was no game-opening jump ball. Instead, the Bulldogs were given the ball out of bounds. Three seconds later, Athens' Mike Croci made a basket on the inbounds play. That made the score 7–0 before the Tigers had even touched the ball.

"The whole game went downhill after that," said Monroe, "I felt bad for the team. As for me, I was rooting for Athens to win by more than seven points." Monroe got his wish. The Bulldogs ripped the Tigers 72–49.

BUTCH ROSS
Quarterback ★ Shawnee Mission (Kansas) South High
Nov. 13, 1981

With five seconds left to play and his Shawnee Mission (Kansas) South High Raiders leading 24–21, quarterback Butch Ross just had to take the snap and fall on the ball to wrap up the win in a big state regional playoff game.

But in his joy over the apparent victory, Ross forgot how to execute football's easiest play.

Ross took the snap at the 40-yard line of the archrival Shawnee Mission West Vikings. He turned and headed toward his own goal to watch the final seconds tick off. Then Ross started shaking hands with his teammates. The cheering South High fans charged out onto the field.

There was no time left on the clock. But there was still enough time for Ross to goof up. He never bothered to down the ball!

West High safety John Reichart was smart enough to know the ball was still in play because Ross' knee had yet to touch the ground. Reichart snatched the ball away from Ross at the 25-yard line and then ran into the end zone for a touchdown. Ross' blunder had turned a sure victory into a stunning 27–24 season-ending defeat. The once-joyful South crowd turned silent in shock as the losing South players hurled their helmets down in disgust.

"I told [Ross] to down the ball," South High coach John Davis ruefully told the press after the game. "I told him to down it, and he didn't do it." What Ross did do was prove that the game is never over until it's over.

WHITE SWAN (WASHINGTON) HIGH VS. HIGHLAND (WASHINGTON) HIGH
Wrestling Match ★ Jan. 28, 1982

It was the weirdest wrestling match in high school history. Not a single takedown or pin. Not a single grunt or groan. That's because the contest between White Swan and Highland turned into a folly full of forfeits.

Both teams had trouble fielding wrestlers in all thirteen weight classes. So no one was surprised when White Swan showed up with only six wrestlers. After all, Highland had just five on hand. What did surprise everyone was something else. None of White Swan's boys and Highland's boys were in the same weight class. That meant no matches could take place.

As a result, the meet was short, sweet—and shameful. White Swan's Donald Weeks stepped forward and the referee declared him the winner by forfeit in the 101-pound class. Next, Highland's Todd Krienke came out and was announced the winner by forfeit in the 108-pound division. And so it went, right up to Highland's Kent Wilkinson who was pronounced the winner—by forfeit, of course—in the unlimited-weight class.

Six points were awarded for a victory in each match. White Swan won the meet 36–30—by virtue of its one extra man.

"We first realized what was happening at the weigh-in," said White Swan coach Lon Henry. "We couldn't do anything but laugh. I only wished we had known ahead of time because the roads were bad [from a winter storm], and we could have called off the match."

At least the fifty or so spectators wouldn't have spent their time and money on 13 matchless matches. Several fans demanded a refund, but Highland High officials refused. They claimed they still needed the gate receipts to pay the referee. Not that he did very much.

"As we were about to leave," said Coach Henry, "the ref came over to me and said, 'This has been the easiest match I've ever had.' You sure couldn't dispute that."

☆

The Hall of Shame of Sports That Don't Have Enough Shame to Have Their Own Hall of Shame

☆

THE WALL GAME
Eton College ★ England ★ 1841–present

If a plaque were given for the worst spectator sport in the world, it would be hung on the Wall Game. Goals are so rare in this strange sporting event that only three have been scored in the last 149 years!

The game is a cross between mud wrestling and soccer. What makes it hard to watch is that the fans rarely know where the ball is. Nor can they tell who the players are once the action begins.

The Wall Game is an annual event played at Eton, the famous English public school. The contest begins at noontime on St. Andrew's Day in late fall. There are two teams of ten Eton lads each. One team is the Collegers, students who live in the dorms. The other is the Oppidans, students who live in town instead of on campus. Their uniforms include jerseys, shorts, and tacky, striped long socks that quickly become soaked with mud.

The playing field usually looks like a boggy moor. It measures 100 meters long and seven meters wide and is bounded on one side by a four-meter-high brick wall. The object of the game is to drive a leather ball through a goal. The ball, which is about half the size of a soccer ball, is kicked along the length of the wall. And the goal is no larger than an ordinary door. No defender may so much as touch the ball in flight. If anyone does, no goal can be scored.

The rules of the game are rather simple and haven't changed much since records were first kept back in 1841. No hands may be used to move the ball. It can only be nudged by feet or knees and cannot be passed from one teammate to another. During most of the game, the players are bunched together in a rugby-like scrum called a "bully."

Those players not in contact with the ball try to push the bully forward. And that's about all the spectators ever see—a grunting, muddy mass of human beings inching back and forth along a wall. It's not exactly the kind of action that makes your spine tingle.

What the fans don't see is what happens inside the bully. The rules forbid kicking, tripping, or punching. They also outlaw "any method of play whose sole purpose is to cause pain." But almost anything else goes as long as it is not "violent or dangerous." There is a referee on hand, but he doesn't do much except make sure no one gets smothered to death. For example, a player on the bottom of the heap may yell "Air!" Then the game stops so he can be rescued.

F.P.E. Gardner, an Eton professor and Wall Game expert, said the contest used to be much more fierce. "Until recently, it was permissible for the players to clench one fist and use their knuckles to gouge the face and eyes of the opponents," he said. "After a particularly rough game, this was outlawed because the Collegers were so disfigured that they could scarcely see out of their bruised eyes to do their university scholarship exams the following day."

Noses still get broken and bodies still get bruised, though. Often, it's by the least likely player. For example, there's "the Fly," who is usually the smallest player. His role is to give a running report on the location of the ball because it has a way of getting lost, even to the players. The Fly makes up in meanness what he lacks in size. He often steps on opponents' hands and uses other tactics that don't seem fair. The Fly, say the rules, may not be swatted.

"No account of the Wall Game would be complete without reference to some of its heroes," said Professor Gardner. "The memory of J. K. Stephen, who played in 1874–76, is toasted every year. He is said to have carried the complete Oppidan bully on his back. Then there was O.W.H. Leeses, who sat on the ball, unmoved in the center of the bully, for over 22 minutes, to prevent a Colleger attack."

Maybe players appreciate such feats, but it doesn't do much for the spectators. Or for the scoring. There hasn't been a goal in more than fifty years. The first one was scored in 1842. The next was in 1885. The last one was over sixty years ago, in 1928. That's an average of one goal about every half century. Is there any doubt that this sporting event is just about pointless?

CHUCK RYAN
Ski Jumper ★ Duluth Invitational ★ Jan. 25, 1959

For ski jumpers, it's always, "Look, Ma, no hands!" For jumper Chuck Ryan, it was, "Look, Ma, no skis!"

Ryan hadn't planned on it, but he set the unofficial record for the longest jump without skis.

More than 2,500 fans were on hand at the time in Fond du Lac, Minnesota, for the 54th annual Duluth Invitational ski jumping championships. What they saw was one for The Sports Hall of SHAME.

Ryan, a nine-year veteran with the St. Paul ski club, should have taken a parachute onto the 60-meter slide. When he hit the takeoff, both his skis flew off his feet. As he soared 148 feet through the air, he cursed himself for using new skis without testing the bindings. Then he told himself to prepare for a rough landing. He hit the snow at an angle, and skidded another 100 feet. Luckily, he came to a stop unhurt.

"I just jumped out of my skis," said the twenty-six-year-old skier. "I wasn't really scared, but I kept thinking that I better not land on my feet and risk breaking my legs. So I went in like a baseball player sliding into second."

The worst shame of all is that no one wrote a song about it. The ditty could have been called, "The Flight of the Bumble Skis."

UNIVERSITY OF MIAMI SWIM TEAM
Feb. 3, 1978

If only the members of the University of Miami swim team had looked before they leaped, the Hurricanes would have swum clear of their poorest pool performance ever.

It happened in a dual meet against the favored archrival University of Florida Gators. The largest crowd of the year was on hand to cheer Miami. Going into the final event, the 400-yard freestyle relay, Miami trailed 54–52. The 'Canes needed to win the relay in order to win the meet.

With fans shouting themselves hoarse, the Miami anchor hit the finish wall in 3:06.05. He barely touched out his Gator rival by just .12 seconds. By winning the race, the Hurricanes had picked up seven points to beat Florida, 59–54. At least, that's what everyone thought—most of all the happy Miami swimmers. Still wearing their sweats and sneakers, they celebrated by plunging into the pool.

Unfortunately, the splash party was a little early—and very costly. Only after the Hurricanes were in the pool did the officials notice the anchor on Florida's outmanned B relay team was still poking along in the water. The Florida finman finally finished, in 3:31.45. Then the partying crowd was silenced by an official announcement.

Miami's swimmers had gone into the water before the race technically ended. So Miami's relay team had broken the rules, and was disqualified. The seven points the Hurricanes had earned were taken away and given to Florida. Miami lost the meet, 61–52.

Similar fates have sunk the fortunes of swim teams before. But no other disaster was as drastic as what happened to the Hurricanes. At the 1971 NCAA championships, for example, Indiana's 800-yard freestyle relay team was disqualified. Swimmers (and future Olympic gold medal winners) Mark Spitz and John Kinsella jumped back into the pool before the race was over. But Indiana had already piled up enough points to win the championship anyway.

Miami had no such extra points to save its victory. "It was quite a shock," recalled Bill Diaz, the Miami coach at the time. "Before the end of any big race," said Diaz, "I always sent one of my assistant coaches to the edge of the pool deck with orders to grab any overly enthusiastic swimmer who looked like he was ready to jump into the pool too early."

ISTVAN GAAL
Canadian National Soccer League Player ★ 1971

Istvan Gaal was such a lousy soccer player that he was traded to a rival team for a ball!

"I think it was a very fair trade," said John Fischer, president of the Kitchener Concordia Kickers of the Canadian National Soccer League. "Both teams got what they wanted."

Gaal was a player whose skills apparently couldn't be measured by money. There was no cash involved in the swap with the Toronto Hungarians. It was a straight player-ball deal.

"We didn't give him away for nothing," Fischer insisted. "We got a regulation National Soccer League ball in return. They go for $27.50."

Long before the trade, Gaal had been considered a prize catch. He was a twenty-one-year-old Hungarian defector who claimed to be a real pro. Gaal said he had scored 31 goals in 44 games back in his native country. As a result, the Kickers went to great lengths to sign him. In fact, they kidnapped him!

Gaal, who had agreed to terms with Toronto, was standing on a Toronto street corner with a team representative. Suddenly, a black car screeched to a halt in front of them. Two men hustled Gaal into the car and roared off to Kitchener. There, he was talked into signing with the Kickers.

"Unfortunately, he turned out to be a big disappointment," said Fischer. "He had a few moves, but he looked bad. At first, we thought he was holding back. He had just arrived in a new country and couldn't speak the language. We thought he'd be okay once he adjusted. But he never improved."

Gaal was so bad that he couldn't even make it as a substitute. And the Kickers were in 13th place in a 14-team league. So a deal was struck with Toronto.

Recalled Fischer, "The Toronto team said to me, 'Why don't you just release the guy to us?' I said, 'No way. I'm not going to give him away for nothing. You send me a soccer ball.' And they did.

"The trade wasn't all that unique," added Fischer. "I went checking through the records and found that a hockey player was once traded for a pair of nets."

LUCKY MAURY
Greyhound ★ Hollywood Greyhound Track
Jan. 19, 1978

In greyhound racing, dogs are trained to dash around the track and chase a fleeing mechanical rabbit that they can never catch. Greyhound Lucky Maury thought all this running for nothing was ridiculous. So he decided to take a different route. He turned tail and ran the opposite way—and ambushed the bunny!

Lucky Maury, running in the fifth race at Hollywood Greyhound Track in Florida, was only a 10–1 shot to win. But after breaking late from the starting box, he looked like a sure loser. He took two gallops on the track and screeched to a halt as if he wanted nothing to do with the doggone event.

But he didn't just give up and head back with his tail between his legs. Instead, the two-year-old racer took matters into his own paws.

Lucky Maury made a U-turn on the track. After he eluded a frantic patrol judge who tried to grab him, the dog scampered off in the opposite direction. At the clubhouse turn, he finally met up with the speeding bunny—head-on. Lucky Maury clamped his jaws on the mechanical rabbit. He ripped it and let the fur fly. When the other dogs caught up, it was hare today, gone to Maury.

The total trashing of the rules made the fans howl with laughter. The track had no choice but to refund all $47,000 that was bet on the race.

Of course, Lucky Maury ended up in the doghouse. A week later, he was put in a nonbetting schooling (practice) race. That was so he could take a refresher course in greyhound-rabbit manners.

WHO ELSE BELONGS IN THE SPORTS HALL OF SHAME?

Do you have any nominations for The Sports Hall of SHAME? Give us your picks for the most shameful, embarrassing, deplorable, blundering, and boneheaded moments in sports history. Here's your opportunity to pay a lighthearted tribute to the world of athletics.

Those nominations that are documented with the greatest number of facts—such as firsthand accounts or newspaper or magazine clippings—have the best chance of being inducted into The Sports Hall of SHAME. Feel free to send as many nominations as you wish for any sport. (All submitted material becomes the property of The Sports Hall of SHAME and is nonreturnable.) Mail your nominations to:

The Sports Hall of SHAME
P.O. Box 31867
Palm Beach Gardens, FL 33420

THE WINNING TEAM

BRUCE NASH has suffered his share of shame in virtually every sport. In his golfing debut, he didn't even make it to the first green—he ran out of balls after shanking eight of them into the water. At the bowling alley, fellow bowlers still talk about the time Bruce threw a wild ball that landed in the gutter—of the next lane.

ALLAN ZULLO has turned his athletic life around. He used to be pathetic and bungling. Now he's bungling and pathetic. As a golfer, he often shoots one under—one under a tree, one under a bush, one under the water. In softball, he's one of the unluckiest pitchers in the park league—Allan always pitches when the other team scores lots of runs.

Hall of SHAME curator BERNIE WARD learned all about shame in high school. He managed to pin himself in a wrestling match when he tripped backward over his own feet.